"Where is she, boy?"

Justice barked, nose pointed toward the park across the street. A stocky figure was rising, a much slighter person in his arms. In the final remnants of daylight, Jared couldn't identify either figure.

But he had no doubt. The woman was Kassie. An unconscious Kassie, judging from the way her arms and legs dangled as the man carried her away.

"Justice, pursue!"

Justice sprang forward as if ejected from a cannon. Jared took off after him, weapon drawn, ready to use if needed.

"Stop! Police!"

The man spun, tossing Kassie away from him. She landed on her side in a crumpled heap. But he was no match for the dog's speed. Justice overtook him in seconds and, in one flying leap, clamped his jaws around the man's forearm.

Rage and pain seemed to erupt from him in an agonized scream.

"Get him off of me!" The assailant fell to his knees and raised his hands. "Call him off."

Justice could hold the man a few seconds longer. He had to check on Kassie.

God, please let her be okay.

Carol J. Post writes fun and fast-paced inspirational romantic suspense stories and lives in the beautiful mountains of North Carolina. She plays the piano and also enjoys sailing, hiking and camping—almost anything outdoors. Her daughters and grandkids live too far away for her liking, so she now pours all that nurturing into taking care of two highly spoiled black cats.

Books by Carol J. Post

Love Inspired Suspense

Visit the Author Profile page at LoveInspired.com for more titles.

Searching for
Evidence

CAROL J. POST

LOVE INSPIRED SUSPENSE
INSPIRATIONAL ROMANCE

LOVE INSPIRED® SUSPENSE
INSPIRATIONAL ROMANCE

ISBN-13: 978-1-335-59814-1

Searching for Evidence

Recycling programs
for this product may
not exist in your area.

Love Inspired
22 Adelaide St. West, 41st Floor
Toronto, Ontario M5H 4E3, Canada
www.LoveInspired.com

Printed in Lithuania

MIX
Paper | Supporting
responsible forestry
FSC® C021394

Nor height, nor depth, nor any other creature, shall be able to separate us from the love of God, which is in Christ Jesus our Lord.
—*Romans* 8:39

Thanks to my sister, Kimberly Coker, for all the plotting help and for keeping this directionally challenged author from getting hopelessly lost during research trips. You're the best sis ever!

Thank you to my editor, Katie Gowrie, and my critique partners, Karen Fleming and Sabrina Jarema, for making my stories the best they can be.

And thank you to my husband, Chris, for your unending love, encouragement and support. You're the inspiration for every hero I write.

ONE

Dead.

Drowned.

No sign of foul play.

Kassandra Ashbaugh stared at the back of her father's Cabo 40 Express sportfisher bobbing in its slip, *Ashbaugh Charters* painted across its transom. Of everyone who'd ever been claimed by the deep, her father was the least likely to be taken that way. He'd been around boats all his life, the past fifteen years as a professional charter captain. He'd been a strong swimmer, too—had even won several medals during his time on his high school swim team.

But two days ago, his boat had been found drifting forty miles offshore, the dinghy still secured and not a soul on board. The throttle was set on low, the gas tanks empty. Fortunately, he hadn't taken any charter customers with him.

Kassie looked past the Cabo at the boat in the next slip. It was also an Ashbaugh vessel, one she'd spent more time on. In recent months, her impossible-to-please father had come to a grudging acceptance of her, but if they'd had to spend the day cooped up on a boat together, one of them might not have come back.

Instead, Kassie got her boating fix twice a week by leaving one of her hairdressers in charge of Kassie's Kuts for a few hours and acting as first mate to their other captain, Buck. He was more of a father figure for her than her own father.

Of course, Buck was usually sober.

She stepped onto the boat and inhaled deeply, drawing in the scent of salt, fish and fresh air. The sun was trying to make an appearance, its top edge barely visible on the horizon. Streaks of orange, pink and lavender stretched outward in both directions, the upper edge fading into semidarkness.

Yesterday, her twin, Kristina, had met the Coast Guard people and completed the necessary paperwork to claim the boat. Kassie's task today was to ready it for Thursday's charter. Between now and then, John, their mechanic, would perform a check of all the systems.

A breeze swept the ends of her ponytail into her face and pressed her lightweight jacket against her back. A shiver shook her shoulders. The April morning air held a little nip, not unusual for the Florida Panhandle.

She raised a hand to greet a boater returning from the Gulf. Seagulls circled him, competing for the bait fish and scraps he tossed overboard. He lifted his arm in a return greeting. So far, they were the only two out and about.

She stepped up into the pilothouse and frowned. Ahead of her, the door going into the cabin area was open. Her father had always kept it closed and locked. Kris apparently hadn't bothered. Or she'd forgotten. Probably the latter.

When their father hadn't returned from his solo outing, Kris had taken it hard. Three days later, the Coast Guard had called off the search, and since then, Kris had alternated between anger and inconsolable grief. All her life, she'd been his favorite, and they'd shared a special bond. Considering Kris's state of mind, Kassie would have met with the Coast Guard folks herself if she hadn't had back-to-back appointments at her salon.

Not that his death had been easy on her. It hadn't, for different reasons.

She descended the four steps and stopped in the galley, arms crossed. It looked like the scene of a small frat party. Besides numerous beer cans, three empty bottles were scattered across the floor. They'd held Jim Beam bourbon.

But there'd been no party. Her father's drinking was never a celebration. It was an escape from whatever disappointments life held.

She heaved a sigh. His drowning wasn't the mystery she had thought it was. Kris hadn't mentioned the empty liquor bottles. Kassie wasn't surprised. Listening to Kris, one would think their father did no wrong. Kassie knew better. Kris did, too. She just chose to live in denial.

The Coast Guard people were right—there were no signs of foul play. What had happened was spelled out in glaring detail right there on the galley floor.

She removed a garbage bag from one of the drawers and tossed in the cans first. A bottle followed, rattling the aluminum. A clunk seemed to echo beyond the galley.

She paused, listening. The early morning was silent except for the call of seagulls and the gentle lap of water against the hull. Soon there was another sound—approaching then fading footsteps. The fisherman had secured his boat and was making his way down the dock.

No one was on the boat with her. The tall, metal gate securing the marina stayed locked. She'd used her key to enter, as would anyone else who wanted to access the area.

She resumed her cleanup. As she added the last two liquor bottles to the trash bag, annoyance surged through her. No, stronger than annoyance—resentment. And a solid dose of anger. Her father's drinking and accompanying fits of rage had cast their shadow over her entire childhood.

Worse, though, was the guilt—regret that she'd never fully

made things right with him, and now he was gone. Her lack of grief only made the guilt worse. What kind of daughter was she, anyway? What kind of Christian?

After finishing the items on the floor, she disposed of a crumb-covered paper plate and plastic knife he'd left in the sink, remnants of making a sandwich. Likely his final meal. A sense of gloom descended over her.

She shook it off and rounded the corner to the head. The face staring back at her from the mirror over the sink bore lines of fatigue. In the coming weeks, it would only get worse. Mounds of paperwork awaited her—starting the process of having her father declared dead in absentia, getting Ashbaugh Charters' records in order, handling the sale of the company. None of it would be easy.

The brief creak of a door hinge sent goosebumps cascading over her. For several seconds, she stood frozen, listening. Again, only the usual seaside sounds surrounded her. But she'd gotten herself spooked enough to consider going topside to see if someone had arrived and would check the boat for her, especially since Kris hadn't locked it. They would find nothing and she'd feel like a wimp, but she didn't have anything to prove.

She stepped from the head and glanced both directions—aft, then fore. A face hidden behind a ski mask peered around the doorway to the front berth.

Her heart jumped to double time, and she leaped toward the steps. As she gripped the handrail, ready to scramble up, heavy footsteps pounded behind her, closing in.

She'd just reached the second step when thick arms wrapped around her waist, holding her in a viselike grip. Her captor jerked her backward, and the railing slipped through her fingers. As he held her aloft, she screamed, long and piercing, kicking at his shins and knees and trying to pry latex-covered hands from her sides.

A second later, he spun in a tight arc and released her. She flailed her arms, eyes wide, as her face moved toward the granite countertop at lightning speed. With a gasp, she turned her head at the last possible second. Her temple slammed into the hard edge, cutting off her final scream midway up her throat.

She landed on the floor in a crumpled heap. The boat tilted. Her assailant had apparently stepped off. Or maybe it was her world that had just tilted.

Shadows hovered at the edges of her vision, then deepened and spread. A ring started somewhere inside her head, competing with the lapping of water and the calls of seagulls. As the ring grew louder, the other sounds faded and disappeared.

The world went dark.

"Come on, Justice. Let's get on the boat."

Jared Miles stepped back from the open door of his Suburban, and his seventy-pound partner shot from the rear seat as if he'd been ejected from a cannon. As a trained police dog, the German shepherd knew a lot of words. *Boat* was one of his favorites.

Jared took a soft cooler from the floorboard and looped the strap over his shoulder. About thirty feet away, someone approached the black metal gate and keyed in the code. Before the gate could swing shut, a second man slipped through on his way out.

As he glanced Jared's way, a sense of familiarity brushed him, accompanied by a jolt of uneasiness. The man was dressed in blue jeans and a gray T-shirt stretched tight over a massive chest and biceps. A zippered pack lay against his back, empty or almost empty, judging from the concave sag of the fabric and the way it bounced.

But it was the man's face that gave him pause. He'd seen him before, and it wasn't in a good capacity. During his twelve

years as a police officer, he'd met a lot of people. This man—
or someone who looked like him—was from far in his past,
near the beginning of his eight-year tenure with Mobile, Alabama, before he'd transferred to Pensacola four years ago.

He shut the Suburban's door and stared after the man as he
walked through the parking lot toward South Barracks Street.
He moved with a relaxed, easy gait. Though nothing about his
actions was suspicious, Jared's uneasiness wouldn't subside.
Whatever contact he'd had with him was buried deep in his
subconscious, but he didn't need the details to remember the
man was coldhearted and cruel. And dangerous.

He looked down at his dog. Justice stared up at him, un-
spoken questions in his dark eyes. With a sigh, Jared walked
toward the marina gate. He couldn't arrest the man when he'd
done nothing wrong. He didn't even have grounds to stop him
and question him.

As he made his way down the dock, Justice trotted beside him, excitement rippling through his black-and-brown
body. They were both ready to enjoy some time on the water.
It might be their last chance for a while. Tomorrow morning,
he'd leave his home in nearby Pace and spend the next several
weeks with his grandmother here in Pensacola. After suffer-
ing a broken hip, having surgery and spending several weeks
in rehab, she was finally coming home.

He made a ninety-degree turn and strode toward the slip
that housed the MasterCraft, formerly his grandfather's boat
but now his. He'd only covered half the distance when Justice came to a dead stop, his body rigid with tension. His ears
went back momentarily, then stood straight up.

"What's the matter, boy? Did you hear something?"

Jared glanced around him. No one was topside on any of the
boats. A forty-foot Cabo occupied the slip he had just passed,
a tuna tower soaring above its Plexiglas-enclosed pilothouse.

He'd seen it moored there before. Based on the words stenciled on the transom, it belonged to a charter company.

Justice's attention was fixed on that boat.

Jared backtracked to stand at its rear corner. The door into the cabin was open. A moan came from inside, likely what Justice had heard.

"Hello? Anyone home?"

In response, he got another groan. Someone was in trouble.

He stepped onto the boat, his holstered weapon hidden beneath his button-up shirt. Likely someone needed medical attention instead of law enforcement. He wouldn't even be considering the possibility of a crime having been committed if he hadn't seen that man walking away from the marina.

When Justice had hopped onto the boat, Jared held out a hand, palm down. "Stay." He'd assess the situation before bringing Justice down.

He stopped at the open door and peered into the galley. A woman was lying on the floor, trying to push herself into a seated position. She winced and pressed a hand to the side of her head.

Jared hurried down the steps and knelt beside her. Blue eyes met his and widened.

He held up a hand. "It's okay. I'm a police officer."

Her gaze flicked to his shirt printed with several types of fish, then took in his khaki shorts and finally his leather boat shoes.

"Off duty. I'm spending the day on the water with my dog."

She met his eyes again, her brow creased.

"What happened? Do you remember?"

"I must have hit my head." She fell silent, as if searching her memory for further details.

"Did you fall?"

"I don't remember."

"What's your name?"

"Kassie. Ashbaugh."

The name on the boat. "Do you remember what you were doing?"

She looked around the galley until her gaze landed on a white kitchen-size bag. "I was cleaning up."

Good. That was a start.

She pulled the bag closer and peered inside. He couldn't see what was there, but judging from the shape of the objects, it held soda or beer cans and two or three bottles.

"We think my dad got drunk, fell overboard and drowned. Coast Guard found the boat. We recovered it yesterday."

She leaned back against the cabinet, eyes closed. That was why she was on the boat, but how did she end up on the floor unconscious?

She didn't appear to have been attacked. Her face wasn't damaged. He couldn't tell whether her arms were bruised under her jacket or jeans. Her dark hair was pulled back in a high ponytail, secured with one of those elastic scrunchie things. Swelling at her left temple was giving her head a slightly lop-sided look. Whether she was injured anywhere else, she needed to have the head injury checked out.

He pulled his phone from his pocket and called dispatch to send an ambulance. Eyes still closed, Kassie raised a hand in a half-hearted attempt to object, an attempt he ignored. He added a request for law enforcement, too, since he wasn't on duty. His gut told him something had happened here other than a fall—something that might have had to do with the man he saw leaving.

He finished the call and pocketed his phone. "So you were cleaning up." It might not be a bad idea to keep her talking in case she had a concussion. "Can you remember anything else?"

Her eyes fluttered open. "I finished the galley area and went to check the head." Her brows creased. "Something happened. I can't—"

She gasped and her jaw dropped. "I heard something. When I stepped out of the head, someone was in the front of the boat."

Likely the man he saw leaving. "What did he look like?"

"He was in a ski mask. Latex gloves, too. I noticed those when he grabbed me."

If it was the same man, he'd discarded both before leaving the marina. Depending on how long Kassie had been unconscious, her attacker may have been someone else entirely.

"Did you notice what he was wearing?"

She started to shake her head, then flinched. "I only saw him for a split second before I ran for the steps. I was so focused on the ski mask, that's all I remember."

The squeal of sirens sounded nearby and grew louder. She drew her brows together, creating vertical creases over her nose. "I've got too much to do to spend the day at the emergency room."

"You need to be checked out."

"Give me a minute. I'll be okay." She pushed herself to her hands and knees and reached up to grip the edge of the countertop. She made it to her feet before swaying sideways.

"Whoa, easy." He put an arm around her and eased her onto the L-shaped bench that wrapped the triangular galley table. "You might have a concussion." He just hoped that was all it was.

She again pressed a hand to her temple and gave him a slight nod.

He held up an index finger. "Don't move. I think the paramedics are here."

When he stepped back onto the deck of the boat, paramedics had already entered their codes and were making their way up the dock. Two police officers approached from the parking lot.

He stepped off the boat, motioning for Justice to follow, and then called to the four men. "Over here."

The paramedics went below, and Jared remained where he was, staying out of the way of the medical folks. Once he gave a report, he and Justice would be free to go.

The two officers approached. He knew them both. The younger, Trey, gave him a nod and a smile. Dave greeted him with a clap on the shoulder. Jared returned the greeting. He and Dave Lazaro had struck up a friendship shortly after Jared had started with Pensacola.

After scratching Justice on the back of the neck, Dave glanced through the companionway door. Their angled view into the cabin offered them little more than the paramedics' backs.

Dave nodded in that direction. "You're the one who called this in?"

"Yep. Justice and I were headed out to go boating and got here as the woman was waking up. She'd been attacked by someone she surprised on her boat."

"Was she able to give you a description?"

"Not really. The guy was wearing a ski mask. That's all she could remember, but she was pretty addled when I talked to her. She might remember more now."

Dave stepped onto the boat, and within moments his bass voice drifted up from the cabin. "Is it all right if I ask the lady a few questions?"

"Sure."

Trey stepped closer to Justice to give him a couple of pats on the back. Since Jared's attention was on the conversation below, Trey stood quietly. Jared was free to go now, but he wasn't willing to leave Kassie until she was on her way to the hospital.

Dave began his questioning. "Can you tell me what happened?"

Kassie related the same details she'd given Jared.

"You told Jared the guy who attacked you was wearing a ski mask. Anything else you can tell us about him? How he was dressed? Height, build?"

"About your size, with big arms. I noticed that when he grabbed me. I still can't remember what he was wearing."

"Any idea who he might have been?"

A short span of silence passed. "About two weeks ago, a guy came on one of Buck's and my charters. He kept watching me. It was…"

Her voice trailed off, and after several seconds, Dave supplied the word. "Creepy? In a lewd way?"

Jared's jaw tightened. Kassie was a pretty girl. He could see some lowlife looking at her like that.

"No. More like… I don't know…like he wanted to hurt me. I know it sounds crazy." She paused. "But something happened when we got back that convinced me I wasn't imagining things."

"Go on."

"My father had come in from a charter just ahead of us and was still at the marina. The guy walked up to him with a swagger, like he was ready to provoke him to a fight or something. They were facing each other, standing less than two feet apart. The big guy was smirking, but my father had his fists clenched and looked ready to tear into him."

"Could you hear them?"

"I couldn't make out the guy's words, but my dad said, 'Stay away from my daughter.' The guy laughed and walked away."

"Did you ask your dad about the exchange?"

"I did. All he'd tell me was that he didn't like the way the guy was looking at me. I should have pressed harder."

"Hindsight's always twenty-twenty." He paused. "Do you keep copies of IDs for your charter customers?"

"We do. I'll call my sister Kris and have her pull that one. I need to tell her what happened anyway."

"Are you taking her to the ER?" He'd directed that question to the paramedics.

"Yeah, Florida West Hospital."

Jared strained to listen for static from Kassie. There wasn't any.

"We'll see you at the ER if we have any other questions."

The paramedic who'd been kneeling in front of Kassie rose. "We'll be back in a minute with a stretcher."

"That's not necessary. I can walk."

The men helped her off the boat and onto the dock. One held her arm, the other walked behind. Her gaze settled on Justice, and her lips curved upward in a soft smile. When her eyes met Jared's, the smile remained.

"Thank you."

He nodded. "Take it easy."

The paramedics continued down the dock with her, but the two officers stayed.

Dave swiped a hand down Justice's back. "Anything else you can add?"

"I saw someone leaving the marina as I was walking up."

Dave's brows rose. "You think it was our guy?"

"Could be. He's a bad dude. We crossed paths when I was a rookie cop with Mobile."

"You got a name?"

"Not one I can pull up at the moment. My involvement was peripheral."

"Anybody you can call for details?"

"I'll work on that."

The most logical choice would be his former partner. But the man was no longer working in law enforcement. Even if he was, Jared would be the last person he'd help.

He'd known going in that he would make enemies. He'd just never dreamed that one of those enemies would be on the same side of the badge.

Dave nodded. "When are you back on?"

"Tomorrow evening."

Jared waved goodbye and watched Dave and Trey head toward the marina's gate. "Come on, Justice. You're finally getting that boat ride I promised."

The dog bounded toward the MasterCraft and leaped on board. After starting the motor and untying from the dock, Jared settled into the captain's chair.

He motored away from the marina with Justice next to him, tail wagging. They wouldn't be back on duty until tomorrow evening, but he had some calls to make. He needed to come up with the identity of the man he'd seen leaving the marina. He'd check with some of his buddies in Mobile.

He never forgot a face. Unfortunately, he couldn't remember the significance of this one. It had been too many years, and he'd worked too many cases since then.

But there was one thing he did know.

If this man was after Kassie, she was in more danger than she realized.

TWO

Kassie stuffed the last of her tuna salad sandwich into her mouth and rose from the table. Usually, dinner was more substantial than this. She was doing well to get that much prepared tonight.

The ER doctor had diagnosed her with a mild concussion and told her to take it easy. Yesterday she'd complied. Today, not so much.

She still had a throbbing headache and a golf ball-sized lump on the side of her head, but she'd been too busy to spend a second day out of commission. So this morning, she'd rolled from the bed and gone to the salon to take care of the six customers who had appointments with her. Then she'd finished readying the boat for tomorrow's charter.

John had checked all the systems, and nothing had been sabotaged. According to Kris, the cops had come by the office, and she'd given them a copy of the charter customer's identification. Hopefully they'd figure out why the man was on the boat, because Kassie didn't have a clue.

After tossing her trash into the bin, she picked up her haircutting kit. She didn't normally do house calls, but if there was anyone she'd make an exception for, it was her sweet elderly neighbor, Ms. MaryAnn. When Kassie had moved into the North Hill Historic District two years earlier, she'd been sold on the quiet neighborhood, the charm of the old house and the view of the park across the street. Having Ms. Mary-Ann right next door had sweetened the deal.

Kassie slipped her purse strap over her shoulder. It didn't matter that she was beat and still had work to do at the charter office. She'd promised Ms. MaryAnn a wash, cut and style when she came home from the rehab center, and she wouldn't disappoint her by rescheduling.

She just hoped her neighbor's grandson wouldn't be there. He was probably a decent guy, since he was moving in to help her out. But for months, the older woman had mentioned him every chance she got, saying what a great fellow he was and that he was single.

Since his grandmother felt the need to find him a woman, he was probably a charity case. Or maybe Ms. MaryAnn felt Kassie was the charity case.

She stepped out the door with her cosmetology tools and turned the key. When she glanced next door, her heart fell. A Pensacola Police cruiser sat in the driveway, smaller print on the door reading "K-9 Unit." Ms. MaryAnn had told her that, too—her grandson was a cop, risking his life daily to keep the residents of Pensacola safe.

Kassie squared her shoulders and marched across the yard. She'd have to meet the man eventually. Might as well get it over with. He couldn't be as persistent as his grandmother.

If he was even interested. After all, guys weren't exactly lining up to date her. It was likely those *not-interested* vibes she'd finally gotten good at putting out. Too bad she hadn't perfected them a few months earlier.

Moments after she rang the bell, the door swung inward. Her jaw dropped. The grandson. Of course he wouldn't make his grandma answer the door. That wasn't what had caught her off guard.

"It's you." The words slipped out before she could stop them. They almost sounded accusatory, as if he should have known they'd soon be neighbors and revealed that fact when they met two days ago on the boat.

His lips curved upward in a relaxed smile. "In the flesh."

He'd looked pretty hot then in his fishing shirt and Docker shorts. He looked even hotter now in his police uniform. His brown hair was no longer lying in haphazard layers, mussed by the breeze. Though still full, it was combed almost flat.

Now, as he looked down at her with laughing brown eyes, a sudden case of teenage shyness hit her. Definitely not a charity case.

But it didn't matter how pleasant he was to look at. After several hard knocks, she'd gotten good at sizing up men. If her vibes said *not interested*, his said, *commitment-phobic*.

Her gaze dipped to the German shepherd standing beside him. His black tail started to wag. She'd seen him Monday, sitting on the dock.

He took a step back. "Come in. Gram said her neighbor was doing her hair tonight." He closed and locked the door. "How's your head?"

"Still a little sore." Still *a lot* sore. Last night, every time she tried to roll onto that side, the pain jarred her awake. Eventually it would fade.

Soft swishes came from the living room. Ms. MaryAnn wheeled her walker toward them, the back legs sliding against the carpet. Her pale blue eyes moved from Kassie to Jared and back to Kassie again.

"I was set to introduce you, but it sounds like someone might have beat me to it."

Jared motioned toward Kassie. "This is the lady I told you about earlier."

"Oh, my!" Ms. MaryAnn turned a scolding gaze on her grandson. "You didn't say the lady you found was Kassie."

"Since you never told me your neighbor lady's name, I didn't make the connection."

Kassie swallowed hard. Great. Her neighbor hadn't just talked to her about Jared. She'd talked to Jared about her.

"Fair enough." She rolled her walker forward to stand almost toe-to-toe with Kassie. "You sure you're okay?"

Kassie smiled. "Positive."

The older woman took a step back to scan her from head to toe and then nodded, apparently satisfied. "You don't look any worse for wear."

"I survived the ordeal quite well."

"God was definitely watching out for you. You could have been seriously injured. Even killed."

"I agree." It *could* have been a whole lot worse. Over the past couple days, she'd thanked God several times for His protection.

As recently as two years ago, she wouldn't have considered giving God credit for anything. Landing in the North Hill Historic District and getting to know Ms. MaryAnn had changed her life in more ways than she could ever have anticipated.

Kassie held out a hand, palm up. "Are you ready to get started on that beauty salon treatment?"

"I've been looking forward to it."

Kassie cast a glance at Jared. "You two are finished with dinner, right?"

Ms. MaryAnn bobbed her head. "We sure are. Jared made baked chicken, mashed potatoes and steamed broccoli. The potatoes weren't those instant things out of a box, either. He peeled 'em, cut 'em up, boiled 'em and mashed 'em. He's a really good cook."

"That's awesome."

Kassie smiled, but Jared seemed to be searching for a place to hide. He'd better get used to it. His grandma wasn't likely to lay off the matchmaking attempts anytime soon.

Ms. MaryAnn made her way to the kitchen, and Kassie followed. The older woman was getting around remarkably well.

Kassie wasn't surprised. Ms. MaryAnn had a strong will and positive outlook to go along with her strong faith.

When they reached the kitchen, Ms. MaryAnn stopped in front of the sink. She'd already placed bottles of conditioner and shampoo and a folded towel on the counter. Or more likely, Jared had.

The older woman released the walker to grip the edges of the countertop and lean forward. Soon her hair was washed, conditioned and toweled dry, and she was sitting in one of her kitchen chairs, a plastic sheet wrapped around her. Perming wasn't necessary. Her silver-gray hair had just enough natural curl to make styling a breeze.

Kassie laid her comb, brush, shears and blow-dryer on the table. Then she set to work combing out the tangles. When she glanced up, Jared was leaning against the doorjamb, watching her.

She grinned. "Are you quality control?"

"Something tells me there's none needed."

She combed a small section of hair between her index and middle finger and picked up the shears. Justice approached and stopped next to her, wagging his tail.

She made a couple of swift cuts and smiled down at the dog. "Hello, sweetie. You're a good boy, aren't you? Pretty boy." The tail wagged harder.

Jared tilted his head to one side. "He might take issue with being called *sweetie* and *pretty*. You're messing with his macho image."

"I don't think he took offense." She laid down the comb to scratch his cheek and throat. "He seems too nice to be a police dog."

"He's a good judge of people. You're not a threat. Besides that, I'm relaxed and haven't given him any aggressive commands. You also like dogs."

"How do you know?"

"Am I right?"

She smiled. "I love dogs. My sister has a golden retriever named Bella, super sweet, awesome with kids. She used to be a search and rescue dog."

"She isn't any longer?"

"My sister's choice, not hers."

"I hope she changes her mind. Working dogs live for what they're trained to do."

"I'm working on her...my sister, that is."

He pushed himself away from the doorjamb. "I have to leave for my shift soon, so I'm going to take this guy out and let you get back to Gram."

It didn't take long for Ms. MaryAnn to ask the question Kassie knew was coming. At least she waited until the front door had closed.

"What did you think of Jared?"

"He's nice."

"And?" She twisted to look up at Kassie with the enthusiasm of a teenager inquiring about her friend's first date. She'd always seemed younger than her seventy-six years. In fact, her broken hip had come from falling on the pickleball court. The first time Kassie had called her Mrs. Struthers, she'd insisted on MaryAnn. They'd compromised with *Ms. MaryAnn*.

"He's good-looking." And well-built. He'd definitely spent some time in the gym, because muscles like that didn't come from operating the TV remote. Those thoughts she'd keep to herself, since whatever she said would likely get back to Jared.

"One of the best-looking guys around, especially in that police uniform. And...?"

Kassie thought for a moment. "He's caring. He was really concerned about me when he found me on the floor of my dad's boat Monday."

"He's always been compassionate. As a kid, he brought home every stray in the neighborhood. And...?"

"I haven't known him long enough to come up with any more *ands*."

"We'll get that remedied soon enough."

Great. There was nothing to remedy. She was quite content with her singleness—no one expecting her to rearrange her life to accommodate his, no one pointing out every perceived shortcoming, no one trying to mold her into his idea of the perfect woman. Like Paul, her ex.

No, single was awesome. But she'd never convince her neighbor of that.

Ms. MaryAnn settled back in for the rest of her haircut. When Kassie finished, she picked up the blow-dryer and a round brush. Soon her neighbor's silvery-gray hair fell in soft, fluffy layers.

Kassie handed her a mirror. Ms. MaryAnn held it up, turning her face slowly side to side.

"Beautiful job, as always."

"I'm glad you're happy with it." She gathered up her supplies and slid them into the zippered bag. "Are you going to be okay here alone?" Based on what Jared had said, he'd be leaving soon also.

"I'll be fine. They wouldn't let me come home from rehab until I could do some things on my own. Besides, I'll be sleeping through most of Jared's shift."

Jared popped back into the kitchen. "Is there anything I can get for you before I leave?"

"No, you kids get on with the things you need to do."

He looked at Kassie. "Can I walk you home?"

"Thanks, but I've got some work to do at the charter office."

He frowned. "You're going out this late?" There was a note of disapproval in his tone.

She looked at him with raised brows. "Is there a local curfew I don't know about?"

"You were attacked two days ago. I'm assuming the guy

responsible is still out there. You might want to watch your back."

She pursed her lips, uneasiness creeping over her. Maybe the guy was only interested in something he thought was on the boat. If that was the case, though, why did her father tell him to stay away from her? Was it even the same man? She sighed. There were too many unanswered questions.

"Thanks, but I'll park on the street, right in front of the office, and lock myself inside. I plan to be out of there before dark."

"I'll drive by a couple of times while I'm patrolling. You'll be taking the burgundy Sorento that's sitting in your driveway?"

"That's right." Kris had picked it up for her Monday afternoon, with a friend's assistance.

After giving her a mock salute, Jared strode to the front door. Justice trotted beside him, exuding excitement.

Kassie headed out behind them. Ten minutes later, she pulled into one of the parallel spaces in front of Ashbaugh Charters. The New Orleans–style building was at the edge of Seville Quarter, one of the historical areas, and less than five minutes from the marina. It had been in her mother's family for years, originally housing her grandfather's real estate brokerage firm.

Kassie glanced around before stepping from the SUV. Traffic was moderately heavy. A handful of people strolled down the sidewalk. In front of her, the sun sat low on the horizon. Daylight would soon fade to night. If she intended to keep her promise to Jared, she needed to be gone within the next half hour.

After she let herself into the building, she relocked the door and disarmed the alarm. The first order of business would be laying out the forms for tomorrow's charter and making sure everything was in order. Previously, her involvement in Ashbaugh Charters had been acting as first mate for Buck. She'd left the clerical end of things to Kris and their dad. But with their dad gone and Kris an emotional mess, that was no longer an option.

She strode to her dad's office, circled behind his antique desk and sank into the swivel oak chair. Directly across from her, an equally old couch sat against the opposite wall. Over the years, her dad had spent more time there than his customers had.

That had been one of her mother's rules—he couldn't come home drunk. Most of the time, he'd complied. Her mom had tried to protect them. Until she decided she'd had enough and took off to the Bahamas with her boyfriend.

Kassie slid open the desk drawer and removed six packets of forms. Tomorrow, after having the customers complete a set, she'd attach a copy of their identification to each one.

Soon the forms sat in a neat stack on the desk. Now to search for whatever accounting records might exist. Tonight's mission was to locate them. Wading through the information would wait till another day.

When she'd asked Kris about the accounting software, Kris had informed her there wasn't any. Their dad had done his own bookkeeping for years and had never computerized anything. Kassie had almost blown a gasket. How was she supposed to sell the company without legitimate financial records?

But she had no choice. She'd kill herself trying to run two businesses, and she'd put too much effort into Kassie's Kuts to consider shutting it down.

Kris was in no position to run Ashbaugh Charters, either. She used to be heavily involved, but she was still reeling from losing her Air Force husband a year earlier and being left to raise their young son alone. She'd cut her involvement in the business down to a few hours a week. Since losing the second most important man in her life, even that was looking iffy.

Their younger sister, Alyssa, would never step up to shoulder any of the responsibility. Besides the fact that she was now living in Atlanta, at least for the time being, her infrequent contacts were only when she needed financial help.

Selling was the only option. When she'd told Kris, it had been Kris's turn to blow a gasket—Ashbaugh Charters was all she had left of her father. Kassie had let it drop. The discussion, not the plans.

She heaved a sigh and searched each of the desk drawers. They produced nothing except a checkbook. Maybe the accounting records were in the file cabinet in the closet. They wouldn't be in the lobby area, and the apartment above the office was out. The last time she'd been up there, it had contained stacks of dusty boxes with contents too old to be of any use now.

She stood up from the chair, and it emitted a protesting creak. At the same time, a rattle came from down the hall. Her breath caught, and she stood frozen, waiting.

The back doorknob jiggled, and her heart stuttered. She grabbed her purse and bounded toward the open door of the office. She'd escape out the front and call the police. The intruder could take anything he wanted. She wasn't about to play the hero.

Before stepping into the hall, she swiped the light switch. At the same moment a splintering boom reverberated through the building, and the rear entrance door slammed back against the hallway wall. Biting off a startled shriek, she retreated into her dad's office. Footsteps pounded closer. She needed somewhere to hide.

She slipped into the closet and pulled the door shut. The file cabinet occupied the right side of the space, with her dad's clothes hanging from a rod on the other side. She slid behind them, pressing herself into the back corner.

The two bathrobes and other clothes had been added long

after her mom's ultimatum, because Kris had laid down the same law. Kassie closed her eyes. Tonight, those clothes might save her life.

The footsteps stopped outside the office door, and she held her breath. *Keep going. Don't come inside.*

The footsteps started again, the heavy tread of tennis shoes against the hardwood floor. The intruder wasn't even trying to be quiet. Of course, there was no reason for stealth. He believed he was alone.

God, please keep it that way.

She peered out from behind the clothes. A sliver of light shone beneath the closet door. The intruder was in her dad's office. Her heart slammed against her rib cage so hard she was afraid he'd hear it.

Had she left any evidence of her presence? Her purse was over her shoulder, her keys inside. So was her phone, but she couldn't risk making noise digging for it. The checkbook lying on the desk wouldn't raise red flags, and she hadn't turned on the lights in the front because it had still been daylight.

Five feet from where she stood, the swivel chair creaked, and she pressed herself more tightly into the back corner. A drawer slid open. Papers rustled. Files hit the floor, and the drawer slammed shut.

Over the next few minutes, the other drawers were emptied the same way. Expletives accompanied the last two.

The chair creaked again as the man rose. When the closet door swung open, her heart almost stopped. *Dear God, help me.*

She held her breath as he emptied the file cabinet the same way he had the desk. Then something slid across the shelf over her head with a long swish. Multiple objects hit the floor in a series of thuds. Whatever he was looking for, he was unhappy not to find it.

Everything grew quiet. But he was still there, inches from

where she hid. His breathing was labored, likely more from anger than exertion.

Then the clothes moved.

Dear God, no. Please protect me.

Instead of sweeping them toward the file cabinet, he pressed them against the side wall, his hand passing right in front of her. The hangers above her head turned at an angle, but the bathrobes kept her concealed.

A ringtone sounded, and she stifled a gasp. A second or two passed before she realized it was coming from outside the closet.

"Yeah." The voice was gruff. After a pause, he continued. "What do you mean she's here?"

Another pause. "Good thing you checked out front again… No, I haven't found anything. Gotta go before she comes inside. Don't wanna have to kill someone tonight."

Footsteps retreated from the room, down the hall and out the back. Kassie sucked in several gasping breaths, suddenly oxygen-deprived.

She needed to get to safety. She couldn't escape out the front, because the other guy might be there. No way was she going out the back, either. Besides, now that the immediate danger had passed, her legs would no longer support her weight.

She slid down the back wall and pulled her phone from her purse. The dimly lit screen warned her of a low charge—the thin red line at the bottom of the battery icon providing confirmation. She just needed time for one quick conversation.

As she lifted the phone to her ear, the flannel fabric of one of the bathrobes swirled around her, the faint scent of cologne the final remnants of the man she'd always called *Dad* but who'd never quite lived up to the name.

THREE

Jared sped down East Government Street, lights flashing. He'd just been dispatched to Ashbaugh Charters for a breaking and entering and was having a hard time keeping his speed to a justifiable level.

Seeing a woman or child in danger had always spurred his protective instincts, but there was something about Kassie that kicked them into overdrive. Maybe it was finding her injured and alone on her boat. Or maybe it was because his grandmother had talked about her so much that he felt as if he knew her.

He drew to a stop behind the burgundy Sorento she'd mentioned earlier and killed the engine. Kassie wasn't waiting out front, and the inside of Ashbaugh Charters was dark. A knot of worry formed in his gut. Where was she?

After stepping from the car, he let Justice out the passenger side. The dog stood next to him as he tried the door into the business. It was locked. The door and jamb didn't show any signs of forced entry. If someone had gained access to the office it wasn't through here.

He peered through the front window, shielding his eyes from the streetlamp behind him. No one stood in the lobby. The darkened hallway appeared empty, too.

He knocked on the French-style wooden door. "Kassie?" No response. He knocked harder. "Police."

This time there was movement in the dark hallway. A figure stepped into the light streaming in through the front window. Definitely Kassie. His neck and shoulder muscles instantly relaxed. As she twisted the dead bolt and swung open the door, her face reflected his own relief.

"I'm so glad you're here." She dropped to one knee and cradled Justice's head in her hands. "Hi, baby boy. You're such a good dog." She spoke with the same singsongy tone she'd used while cutting his grandmother's hair.

Justice wagged his tail so hard, his back end swayed. He'd been without a woman's touch for too long and was eating up the attention Kassie gave him.

She straightened and pointed behind her. "He broke in the back and rummaged through my dad's office while I hid in the closet. Then he went out the same way he came in. Maybe Justice can follow the trail."

"He's not a search and rescue dog like your Bella."

Even while he voiced his objection, Jared rushed past her and down the hall. Justice couldn't compete with Bella's tracking skills, but he had some knowledge. Trainers had tried him with search and rescue before discovering his toy drive wasn't strong enough and he was better suited to police work.

The hallway light came on, and Kassie approached from behind. He glanced through an open door on the left—likely the office she'd mentioned. Someone had ransacked the place, slinging papers, files and office supplies everywhere.

Kassie stopped next to him and pointed. "He sat there."

Jared stepped around the objects strewn on the floor and led Justice to the chair. "Let's go find him, buddy."

He followed the dog out of the office and down the hall. The door at the end was wide open, hanging lopsided on its hinges. Justice loped into the small parking area that backed the building. After stopping and sniffing the air, he proceeded right a few yards and looked back at Jared.

"What's wrong, buddy?"

The dog trotted back and stood in front of him. He'd apparently lost the scent. Maybe the intruder got into a car there. Or maybe Justice hadn't zeroed in on the right smell after all. His search abilities were more reliable at some times than at others.

When Jared stepped back inside, another unit had arrived, and Kassie was in the lobby speaking with one of his fellow officers, Steve Foster. She flashed a smile in their direction before returning her attention to Steve.

"I didn't see him, because I was hiding in the closet, but he sounded like someone who took one of our charters." She told him about the attack on the boat, ending with the interaction with the customer.

Steve nodded. "We'll try to lift prints."

When he left to retrieve his fingerprint kit, Jared approached her. "You said you had a copy of the charter customer's ID."

"Kris made a copy of it and gave it to the police."

"Can I see?"

"Sure."

He watched Steve walk back through with his kit. "We'll wait until he's finished."

Fifteen minutes later, Kassie brought him into the office and sat on the floor to pick through the files and loose papers scattered about.

Finally, she held up a stapled stack. "Bingo. This is the paperwork for that charter." She stood and flipped through several pages. "Here he is."

Jared pressed his lips together. The photo matched the man he saw leaving the marina. When he looked back at Kassie, she was studying him.

"You recognize him." It was a statement rather than a question. She was perceptive.

"He was leaving the marina as I was arriving."

"We've got his name and address, and you can place him

at the marina when I was attacked. So you guys can arrest him, right?"

"We can bring him in for questioning. We need a little more evidence to arrest him."

She drew her lower lip between her teeth. "He was wearing gloves, so there won't be fingerprints."

"First, we'll find out what he was doing there." He looked back down at what she held. Definitely the guy he saw leaving the marina, the same man he'd encountered as a rookie cop. The license even had a Mobile, Alabama address, further convincing him that Kassie had gotten embroiled in something dangerous.

"Can you copy this for me? I'd like to do my own checking."

"Sure." She led him back out to the lobby, where she did as he'd asked.

"Thanks. I'll let you know what I find out." He paused. "Are you headed home now?"

"I need to get the office cleaned up, at least get the stuff off the floor."

"Can't it wait till tomorrow?"

She shrugged. "I could take care of the charter paperwork in the lobby instead of in here. I need to secure the back door, though."

"I'll look at it with you." Since he was on duty, he couldn't repair it properly, but anything would be better than leaving it wide open.

He followed her back down the hall, Justice at his heels. She wrestled the door most of the way shut, but the jamb was too damaged for it to close completely.

She turned toward him. "There's a small tool kit in the hall closet. I think if I hammer the splintered jamb together, the damage won't be obvious from outside."

He pressed himself against the wall to allow her to pass. A faint fruity scent wafted up to him, probably some type of hair product. She was a whole head shorter than he was, small-framed and in decent shape. Maybe her small stature helped feed that sense of protectiveness he felt around her.

Once she'd retrieved a hammer, she returned. A few blows had the splintered pieces lined back up enough to allow the door to clear.

She turned toward him with a confident smile. "If someone rammed it hard, it would give way, but no one wandering through the parking area would know."

"Just in case, is your cash secure?"

"Locked in the safe. I'll have the door fixed tomorrow. Meanwhile, the alarm will be set. I didn't arm it earlier because the motion sensor would have detected my movement and triggered the alarm."

"You have an alarm at home, too?"

"I do."

"Monitored?"

"Yes."

"Good. I guess you're heading that way?"

"After one stop. My sister left her Yeti tea mug here. I promised I'd drop it by so she wouldn't have to bring her son, Gavin, out." She grinned. "I take any opportunity I can to love on that little boy."

He smiled at the affection in her eyes. "What about doing that tomorrow morning, after daylight?"

"It'll make my schedule a little tighter, but I can make it work. I just need to call her. She was expecting me thirty minutes ago."

She pulled her phone from her purse and frowned. "I'll have to use the office phone."

Glancing at the black powder coating everything, she forwent the chair and stood next to the desk. Jared stepped into the hall to wait.

After relaying the scary events to her sister, she promised

to be there in the morning. She fell silent, and when she spoke again, there was sadness in her tone.

"I'm sorry. Tell him his aunt Kassie will bring him something special tomorrow."

She finished the call and stepped into the hall. "My nephew is having a hard time with losing his grandfather. Kris said he keeps going into his room, looking for him."

"He lived with them?"

"Technically, they lived with him." She moved toward the front. "When Kris's husband was killed in a car accident a year ago, my dad asked her and Gavin to live with him. She agreed on one condition: No drinking around either of them. He couldn't even be under the influence. He agreed." She switched off the hall light. When she continued, her tone held hardness. "Looks like he took up drinking on his boat instead."

After arming the alarm system, she stepped outside. "Gavin was really close to him. My dad made a better grandpa than father."

"How is your mom handling it?"

"Probably fine." That hardness was back. "She took off ten years ago, and we haven't heard from her since."

"That's rough." Not that he could relate. His parents were awesome. After thirty-five years, they were still together, and he was close to both of them.

He walked her to the driver door of the Sorento. "Is there somewhere else your sister can go?"

"I don't know. Why?"

"Someone came on the boat and broke into the charter office. If this has anything to do with your father, his home might be next."

Kassie frowned, worry creases appearing between her eyebrows and around her mouth. "I didn't think of that. I'll talk to her."

"Meanwhile, I'll request that units drive by, keep an eye on the place."

She gave him the address, and he saved it in his phone.

"Not trying to pry, but the *something special* you promised your nephew—that won't require a trip to the store tonight, will it?"

"No. His second birthday is next week. I'll give him one of his presents early."

Before getting into the car, she smiled up at him in the glow of the streetlights. The hardness in her tone hadn't made it to her eyes. The blue appeared deeper than in daylight, and they seemed to spark with a touch of humor. "I'm glad it was you who responded. Although you're making a habit of rescuing me. I'm still trying to decide how I feel about that. I'm usually not one who needs to be rescued."

Yeah, she didn't strike him as helpless or needy. According to his grandmother, she was pretty amazing—owned her own hairstyling salon, helped out with her father's charter business, came over to play games on a regular basis and played the piano like a master.

"Not a problem. Guys like to be rescuers." He grinned. "Must be those fairy tales our moms read us when we were little."

After she slid into her driver's seat, he closed her door and walked to his cruiser. He'd follow her a short distance. Once he was sure no one was tailing her, he'd stop to make some phone calls.

A few blocks from her home, he pulled into a convenience store parking lot. Dave or Trey would have already run the license of the charter customer. No sense duplicating efforts.

He slid his cell phone from his pocket. Once he put the call through, he looked at the sheet of paper in his hand. Hector Wescott. It didn't ring a bell, but he'd always been better with faces than names.

After three rings, Dave answered.

"I know you're off." At least it wasn't the middle of the night. "That call Monday at Seville Harbour Marina, you guys got a copy of the charter customer's driver's license, right?"

"We did. Dead end. It's fake."

He heaved a sigh. They were back to square one—no information on the suspect and nowhere to even begin looking. He filled Dave in on tonight's events and disconnected the call. One more person to phone.

Ever since seeing the man leaving the marina Monday, Jared had tried to jog his memory. He was still coming up as blank as he had when he'd first seen the guy.

He scrolled through his contacts again. Samuel Schwartz wasn't just a longtime partner at Mobile PD. Sam and his wife had become Jared and his late wife's best friends.

After greeting his buddy, Jared got to the reason for his call. "I need to pick your brain."

"All right, pick away."

"I'm trying to remember information on a suspect from more than ten years ago."

"What kind of case?"

"I don't remember. I think I was present for the arrest, but others took it from there."

"Name?"

"I don't remember. He's used the name Hector Wescott recently."

"Description?"

"Caucasian, between thirty-five and forty, about five-ten, maybe six foot. Built like a linebacker for the Crimson Tide. I'll email you his driver's license. The name's an alias, but you'll have the photo."

"Who were you working with?"

"Silas Beechum."

"Oh." The word was heavy with meaning. When Jared

started, Sam had already been with the department a couple of years. Like everyone else there at the time, Sam was well aware of the details that had brought down the veteran law enforcement officer, as well as Jared's part in those events. To some, he was a hero. To others he was a snitch and traitor. He hadn't set out to be either.

"Anything else you can tell me about this guy?"

"I wish I could."

"I'll see what I can find out."

"Thanks."

"Jared?"

"Yeah." He knew what was coming.

"How are you doing?" It was the same question Sam had asked for the past two years. He was never looking for the pat answer "fine" and wouldn't let Jared get away with saying it, no matter how much Jared might want to.

"I stay busy, but it's still tough sometimes. Staying with Gram helps."

"I'm sure. Solitude can make for some serious loneliness." He paused. "I'm still praying for you, buddy."

"I appreciate it."

When his world had caved in, it was prayer that had kept him afloat. Not his own. Those lifesaving prayers had come from friends like Sam, his mom and dad, and people in his and Miranda's church. Although, since Miranda had usually attended alone, he wasn't being honest if he claimed the church as his own. When Sunday mornings had rolled around, he'd never been short on excuses. One more thing to add to his present-day regrets.

"I'll let you know if I learn anything about your mystery guy."

After thanking him again, Jared disconnected the call, shaking off a sudden sense of melancholy. He had a job to do and part of that job was trying to secure the safety of Gram's pretty neighbor.

Finding out the identity of her attacker through the channels he was using really was a long shot. Those who'd been with the department then had handled dozens of cases since. The odds of remembering a single one, especially if they weren't directly involved, were slim to none. Sam would do what he could, but Jared wasn't holding out much hope.

Everyone willing to provide the information probably couldn't.

And the one who probably could wouldn't.

Kassie parked her SUV in front of the huge old house where she'd grown up. Although in need of some TLC, it was still beautiful.

She picked up the Yeti mug and a box wrapped in colorful paper. What was supposed to be a brief delivery had turned into an invitation to breakfast, something Kassie never turned down when her twin was involved.

When she'd gotten home last night, she'd called Kris back to express Jared's concerns. As far as leaving, Kris said she'd think about it. Between her dog and her security system, as well as the extra police protection, she hadn't been sure it was necessary.

Kassie stepped from the Sorento, purse hanging from one shoulder and mug and gift clutched against her chest. The house in front of her was Victorian, without the gingerbread. Her great-grandparents had had it built at the turn of the last century. They'd passed it down to her mom's parents, who'd passed it down to her mom.

It was still in her mom's name. Her dad had never been able to transfer the deed. He couldn't have her declared dead, because she was very much alive. The typed note she'd left proved it. It detailed exactly why she left—she could no longer tolerate living with an alcoholic husband. The airline ticket she purchased to fly her from Pensacola to Grand Bahama International Airport was further proof. No one knew where she went after arriving in Freeport. She hadn't spoken to anyone since she left. That day, she walked away from all that had made up her life—her faith, her home, her husband and her daughters.

Kassie headed up the sidewalk leading to the front porch. Its borders were now bare. The annuals that had lined the curved concrete path the last time she'd been there were gone. Kris was likely preparing to do her spring planting.

Any activity was a move in the right direction. For the past week, Kris had been in such a funk that Kassie had been worried about her. Other than meeting the Coast Guard people and stopping in twice at the charter company, she'd stayed cooped up in the house. Getting some sunshine and fresh air would be good for both her and Gavin.

Kassie stepped onto the porch that wrapped two sides of the house and knocked on the front door.

Her sister responded from inside. "Come in."

As she pushed the door inward, pleasant aromas wrapped around her. Her stomach rumbled in response. Kris's breakfast casserole was to die for. All of Kris's cooking was to die for. It was the one domestic activity their father appreciated, because he liked to eat. So while Kassie had immersed herself in Mozart and Beethoven, Kris had thrown herself into perfecting dishes like turkey roulade and crème brûlée.

Kassie closed the door, and little footsteps pattered toward her. Gavin rounded the corner and slammed into her, wrapping his arms around her knees

"Aunt Kassie!"

Kassie disentangled herself to drop to a squat. "Aunt Kassie brought you something."

As soon as she handed him the box, he set to work on the wrapping paper. Bella padded into the entry, not about to miss out on the action. While Kassie watched Gavin unwrap his gift, she scratched the golden retriever behind the ears.

Gavin tossed the paper to the floor. "A twuck."

"It's a dump truck." She wadded up what he'd discarded and lifted him from the floor. One little arm went around her neck. The other hand still clutched the truck. When they stepped into the kitchen, Kris was standing in front of the oven.

"Mommy, look!" He held up the prize.

Kris spun with a smile. "Wow, Aunt Kassie brought you a dump truck. What do you say?"

"Tank you."

Kris removed a casserole dish from the oven and placed it on top of the stove.

Kassie inhaled deeply, the scents hitting her full force. "Man, that smells good."

"Payment for bringing me my mug."

"I'll play delivery driver anytime."

Kris grinned. "I'll keep that in mind."

After throwing the wrapping paper into the trash, Kassie strapped Gavin into his high chair. He rolled his truck back and forth across the tray as his mother bustled about the kitchen. She seemed to be in a good mood. Maybe she was coming to terms with their father's disappearance. Or maybe she'd decided to push aside her own sadness for Gavin's sake.

She'd done it once before—forged ahead when she'd felt like giving up. That had been for Gavin's sake, too. The little boy had no idea what a blessing he was.

Kris brought the food to the table and took the chair next to her son. Kassie sat opposite them, and the toddler folded his hands. He knew the routine, at least when his aunt was there.

After Kassie had finished her simple prayer, Gavin added his own hearty *Amen*.

Soon plates were filled with food, and the stack of buttered cinnamon bread in the center of the table was almost empty.

The truck sat a short distance away, having been relocated with only minor fussing from Gavin.

Kris picked up her fork. "After breakfast, Gavin and I are going out with Shannon on her boat." When she continued, her voice held a note of defensiveness. "I need some time away, even if it's just for a few hours."

"I agree." Maybe that was behind Kris's good mood. Having something to look forward to, even just spending the day with a friend, could work wonders on lifting one's spirits. "I hope y'all have a wonderful time."

She meant what she'd said and didn't want Kris feeling guilty. Eventually she'd be able to shoulder her share of the responsibilities.

Relief flashed across Kris's features. "Thank you. Shannon is really good at cheering me up."

Kassie had to agree. Shannon, with her carefree, can't-tie-me-down attitude, and Kris, with her determined, sometimes too serious personality, had always seemed the most unlikely of people to forge a lasting friendship. But maybe it was their differences that made them so compatible.

Kris continued. "Sometime soon, I'm stopping at GTF Nursery to pick up some plants."

"Good."

Kassie took a bite of cinnamon bread, relishing the sweetness. Eventually, she'd again broach the subject of selling Ashbaugh Charters. What to do with the house was another decision that would have to be made. Without a clear deed, selling it wasn't an option. There was no mortgage, but between the home's value and its location right on the bayou, taxes and insurance were probably astronomical, plus the cost of upkeep. If they couldn't afford the expenses, they'd have to lease part of it out. But those were discussions for another time.

Gavin reached toward the center of the table. "More toas', pease."

Kris scooped up a bite of casserole with his fork. "Let's eat some eggs first."

"'Kay." He opened his mouth and Kris shoveled in the bite.

When she handed him the fork, he took the next mouthful without encouragement. He'd always been a compliant child. It was a blessing since she was raising him alone.

She shifted her attention to Kassie. "Have you heard anything from the police?"

"Just that the driver's license the guy gave us was fake. So we have no information on the charter customer."

Kris sighed. "I was afraid of that."

"The guy who attacked me on the boat was the right size, but I never saw his face or heard him speak. The one who broke into the office last night had the same deep, gravelly voice the charter customer did, but I don't know what he looked like."

"Any idea what he was searching for?"

"Not a clue. Did Dad ever say anything?"

Kris's eyebrows drew together over eyes filled with suspicion. "About what?"

"Did he ever say anything that seemed a little... I don't know, odd?"

"What are you insinuating?"

"I'm not insinuating anything. But someone is searching for something, and they believe it's hidden on the boat or in the office. Is it possible Dad might have been involved in something we don't know about?"

"Like what?" Each question held more indignation than the last.

"I don't know. I was hoping you might be able to figure this out. You've always been more involved in the business than I have." At least until the past year. "Maybe he has something that belongs to the man."

"Now you're calling him a thief?" Kris slammed her hand down on the table. "I won't let you dishonor his memory."

Gavin started to cry, and Kris patted his shoulder. "It's okay, sweetie. Mommy and Aunt Kassie are just talking."

Kassie sighed. She and her twin had always seemed to have a love-hate relationship. As they'd established themselves as successful adults, the friction between them had gradually subsided. But it didn't take much for old resentments to bubble to the surface.

"I'm not dishonoring his memory." But she wasn't wearing the same blinders her sister was. "I'm just asking you to try to figure out what Dad might have had that someone would be this desperate to get their hands on."

Kris picked up her fork again. "I'll think about it."

"That's all I'm asking."

At least the discussion didn't get ugly, not like their exchanges had as children. When they were growing up, the competition between them had been fierce—in school and at home. It didn't help that their dad hadn't even tried to hide his favoritism. Kassie couldn't please him and Kris could do no wrong. Alyssa didn't even try.

Their mom hadn't had a favorite. She'd treated them equally. Then she'd walked out, taking her flute and some personal possessions and leaving her daughters. What kind of pathetic excuse for a human being would walk away from her children and never speak to them again?

Kris sat back in her chair and crossed her arms. "I don't think this has anything to do with Dad. I think you're the one the guy's after."

"Me?"

"Yeah. If not, why did Dad warn the guy to stay away from you?"

Kassie frowned. She'd told Kris about the exchange right after it had happened. "I don't know."

"You said he kept watching you, right?"

A knot formed in her stomach. Kris had a point. She was involved in this whether she wanted to be or not.

Kris shrugged. "It sounds like he might have been a little obsessed."

"But why risk going on the boat?"

"Because that was where he spent the day with you. Maybe he was wanting to be where you'd been, to touch the things you'd touched. Which boat were you on for that charter?"

"We'd taken the Cabo that day."

"So it's possible."

No, that wasn't the way he'd looked at her. But a shudder shook her shoulders anyway.

Kris continued. "Are you keeping an eye out, making sure no one's following you?"

"Probably not as diligently as I should."

"You need to keep your eyes open."

Yeah, she usually did. She wasn't one to take walks wearing earbuds. When going in and out of stores, she looked around her, ever alert. And she'd never taken unnecessary risks, under any circumstances. But she still wasn't buying Kris's theory.

"The man who broke into the office was looking for something. I don't have anything in either place. I haven't even left a spare sweater."

"Maybe he was looking for your file."

"What file?"

"Your employment documents, like your I-9. That would have your home address on it."

The knot in her stomach grew. Could that really be what the intruder was searching for, a way to get to her?

No, Kris was grasping at straws. Anything to shift blame from their father. If it made her feel better, fine. Kris could take comfort in her delusions. The truth would come out eventually.

Whoever the man was, he wasn't after her personally.

She was attacked on the boat because he was there when she boarded. And when he broke into the office, he had no knowledge she was inside. Both times she'd been in the wrong place at the wrong time. No one meant her any harm.

If that was true, why was her father so upset at seeing the man on her and Buck's charter? And why did he warn him to stay away from her?

Maybe *she* was the one trying to take comfort in delusions.

FOUR

Jared pulled into a space at Ever'man Market, his grand-mother's grocery list and a pen in his shirt pocket. Three green cloth bags with the Ever'man logo sat in the seat beside him. It was the local organic market, with its own café, and his grandmother's favorite place to shop.

He killed the Suburban's engine and slid from the seat, swiping the bags on his way out. A couple of spaces away from where he'd parked, a burgundy Sorento occupied a slot, its Ashbaugh Charters bumper sticker identifying it as Kassie's.

He smiled. If he didn't know better, he'd guess Gram had something to do with the two of them being there at the same time. He wouldn't put it past her.

For a good six months, she'd talked about her neighbor, what a sweet girl she was, single, close to his age. Most importantly, she was a Christian. Since he'd renewed the commitment he'd made as a child and had finally gotten serious about his faith, that attribute was non-negotiable. Or it would be if he was looking. He wasn't.

He snagged a cart and pulled his grandmother's list from his pocket. It was pretty lengthy, considering there were only two of them. Maybe she planned to have Kassie join them reg-ularly. He wouldn't object. Sam was right. Solitude made for some serious loneliness. If his friendship with Kassie helped ease some of that, Gram could have her over anytime.

But that was all he would consider—friendship. Kassie seemed nice, and he'd have to be blind to miss how attractive she was. She was talented, ambitious, likable, fun to be around. None of it mattered. He didn't plan to remain single the rest of his life, but as long as the image of Miranda's crumpled form at the edge of the road haunted his dreams, he was nowhere near ready to move on.

He glanced at the list. He'd start on the far side of the store and save the produce for last. As he walked the aisles, he sought out women with dark ponytails. He couldn't help it. It was how Kassie had worn her hair every time he'd seen her.

Three aisles later, he turned the corner to find her leaning toward a shelf, studying a selection of condensed soups. She was dressed in a T-shirt and modest shorts, skin bearing a healthy glow, as if she'd spent the day in the sun. A high ponytail hung from an elastic band.

He stopped his cart next to her. "Any brand you'd recommend?"

She picked up a can of cream of mushroom soup. "This makes great—" As she made eye contact with him, a slow smile spread across her face. "Oh, hey."

"Hey yourself. How did your charter go?"

"It went well."

"No creepy guys?"

"Not a one."

"I take it your sister's mug is in its proper location?"

"Yep. I even got breakfast out of the deal."

"Cool. Did you talk to her about staying somewhere else?"

"I did last night, but I don't think she's planning to leave. She's comfortable with the dog and her alarm. Besides, she thinks the break-ins have to do with me instead of Dad."

"How?"

"She thinks the charter guy was obsessed with me and broke into the office looking for my information." She moved down the aisle, still talking. "I don't suppose the police have learned anything about who he is."

He smiled at her. "Since last night?"

She returned his smile. "I guess it doesn't work like it does on CSI, where everything is wrapped up in one hour-long episode."

"'Fraid not."

For the next fifteen minutes, he continued through the aisles with Kassie, filling his cart with the final items on Gram's list. After checking out, he stepped from the store, Kassie ahead of him. She looked around, then stiffened.

He followed her gaze. A Honda Acura was parked at the edge of Garden Street, bordering the north side of the store. A man sat slouched in the driver's seat, a ball cap pulled low on his head.

"What is it?"

"That guy over there." She indicated him with a tilt of her head. "I'd think he was waiting for someone, but as soon as I looked his way, he slid down and pulled the bill of his cap over his eyes."

"Go back inside."

When she had complied, he ambled along the front of the store, trying to not spook the driver. He'd covered less than five yards when the car's engine rumbled to life. The next moment, the driver shot away amid the squeal of tires, disappearing past the corner of the building.

Jared ran to the street and down the sidewalk, squinting at the back of the car. It bore a Florida tag. After reciting the combination of letters and numbers aloud twice, he stopped to pull Gram's grocery list and pen from his pocket.

Once he had the information recorded, he jogged back toward the store. As he'd instructed, Kassie was waiting inside. She'd pulled his cart in also and was standing between them.

She stepped out, pushing hers and pulling his behind her. "Did you talk to him?"

"No. As soon as I headed toward the street, he took off like he'd just robbed a bank. Definitely up to no good."

Kassie frowned. "Do you think he was the same guy you saw leaving the marina?"

"I don't know. I didn't get a good look." He held up Gram's grocery list. "I did get a tag number, though."

Her eyes lit up. "Can you run it now?"

"I'll call it in as soon as I get to my truck."

"Where are you parked?"

"Two spaces beyond you."

"I'll meet you there once I get my groceries loaded."

He'd just finished putting the filled cloth bags into the back seat when she stepped up beside him.

He opened the passenger door. "Get in. I'd rather you not stand outside."

Once he'd slid into the driver's seat, he called Dave and soon had a name and address. He disconnected the call and looked at Kassie.

Her eyes were lit with excitement. "Can we go there now?"

"There's no *we* to it. You need to stay as far away from this guy as possible. Besides, there are detectives assigned to the case. I'm turning this over to them."

"This is good, though, right? I mean, having a name and address, that's like a huge break."

"If it's the same guy." He didn't want to give her false hope. "Neither of us got a good look at him, so we can't be sure. But we'll check him out. In the meantime, you need to keep up your guard."

"I am. That's good to do even if you're not being stalked. Especially as a woman."

"Very true."

Kassie was sharp. He couldn't count the number of times

he'd seen a young woman walk through a parking lot, head down, eyes glued to her phone.

She opened the door and slid from the truck. "Thanks for shopping with me and for checking out the car. Maybe that name and address will lead us somewhere."

He stepped from the driver's seat and met her at the back of the Suburban. "I assume you're heading home now, since you've got groceries."

"I am."

"I'll follow you."

"You don't need to go to the trouble. It's still daylight. I'm sure I'll be fine."

He tilted his head to the side. "Since I've got my own groceries, I'm heading home, too. Currently, that happens to be right next door."

She grinned. "You've got a point."

They'd almost reached her vehicle when her phone rang. She pulled it from her purse and glanced at the screen.

"It's my sister. I'll tell her I'll call her back when I get home."

She swiped the phone and put it to her ear. Before she had completed her "Hello," shrill words poured through the phone, although he couldn't make them out.

Kassie's eyes widened. "Kris, I can't understand you. What's going on? Is Gavin all right?"

The response didn't seem quite as hysterical, but Kassie was just as tense. "Call the police. I'm heading there now."

She disconnected the call and looked up at him. "I have to go. Someone ransacked my sister's house."

"I'm following you." He had time before his shift. "I'll see you there." He moved toward his SUV at a jog.

He wasn't on duty. Others would respond.

But whatever was going on, the two women didn't need to face it alone.

* * *

Kassie turned onto Cross Street and once again stepped on the gas. Hearing the fear in Kris's voice had sent panic shooting through her. When Gavin had started to cry in the background, it had just about put her over the edge.

It was bad enough that her father might have done something to put *her* in danger. Over the past three days, she'd alternated between fear, confusion and anger. But if he'd risked that innocent little boy's life—that was inexcusable. What if Kris and Gavin had been there when the intruder came in? *Thank you, God, that they're safe.*

When she approached the driveway, a Pensacola Police cruiser was sitting behind Kris's red CR-V. The officers had apparently just arrived. They stepped from the vehicle as Kassie stopped along the edge of the road. Jared pulled over behind her. He'd stayed right on her tail the entire ten-minute drive there.

Kris exited the Honda's driver's seat. When she opened the back door, Bella jumped to the driveway, tail wagging. They'd waited in the car. Probably a smart decision, not knowing whether someone was still inside. Or maybe not if that someone was outside watching.

Kassie sprang from her SUV and ran to Kris, who was helping Gavin from the car. She scooped up her nephew and wrapped him in a tight hug. His arms went around her neck.

One of the officers approached, and Kris addressed him. "My son and I were gone all day. When we got home, the front door was locked, and everything looked normal. The alarm was even still set. When I opened the door, I had to punch in the code. But I knew someone had broken in. I didn't go beyond the foyer, but from what I could see, the place has been ransacked."

The officer nodded. "How many people have the security code?"

"Besides me, just my sister and my dad."

At the sound of footsteps behind her, Kassie turned to see Jared approaching. He stopped next to her, and the officer greeted him by name. When Jared's gaze shifted to Kris, he did a double take. "You guys must be twins."

"We are." They answered in unison.

They could never disown each other. They looked too much alike, even though they sported different hair styles. Always the tomboy, Kris's hair had never brushed her shoulders. She'd worn it in bob-type dos since being given the choice in early grade school. Kassie's had always been long.

Jared patted Gavin on the back. "And this must be that little boy you're so crazy about. Hey, buddy."

Kassie gave him a broad smile. Good with kids—a character trait Ms. MaryAnn had missed all the times she'd sung his praises.

The officer motioned toward the front door. His name plate said Bloom. Jared had called him Tyler. "My partner and I will go inside and make sure everything is secure. Wait here with Jared."

The two officers disappeared through the front door. When they stepped back out several minutes later, the younger officer announced that he would check the exterior and Bloom approached them.

"Everything's clear. You can come inside and tell me if anything appears to be missing."

Kris led him up the front walk, with Kassie following, still carrying Gavin. Bella padded ahead, excited to be home, and Jared brought up the rear. Usually, Gavin was too full of energy to allow anyone to hold him for long. Not today. He was clinging to Kassie as tightly as he had when she'd first picked him up.

Kassie tightened her hold on him, a wave of emotion sweeping through her. Kris needed to get them all somewhere safe.

Staying in the huge family home, with its large windows and French doors across the back wasn't an option.

When Kassie stepped into the house, her heart fell. The drawers of her mother's Bombay chest were pulled out and tossed on the floor, their contents strewn about the foyer. To the right, a large open doorway revealed the living room in even greater shambles. Everything was pulled off the shelves. Couch cushions were scattered about the room, stuffing protruding from long slashes.

As Kris led them through the spaces, Bella sniffed the mess and Officer Bloom took pictures. When they entered the kitchen, the back door was slightly ajar, a pane of glass broken out.

Bloom snapped another picture. "There's where he gained entry."

"Why didn't opening the door trigger the alarm?"

"He blocked the sensor."

Kassie moved closer with Kris. A piece of duct tape covered a small section of the door stop, a bulge beneath it.

Bloom continued. "Depending on the sensitivity of an alarm, an intruder might be able to slowly open the door enough to slide a popsicle stick or credit card into the opening and keep the button depressed until he can get it blocked."

He stepped back. "Let's look at the rest of the house."

After checking upstairs, they returned to the first floor. Not a single room was untouched. Kris leaned against a doorjamb, shoulders slouched, face pale.

Kassie put Gavin down and wrapped her arms around her sister. "We'll get it cleaned up. I'll help you."

Kris returned the hug, but it felt stiff. They'd never had that kind of relationship. In fact, Kassie could count on the fingers of one hand the number of times they'd embraced. Once was at Kris and Mark's wedding. Another was when Mark was killed.

There'd been no hugs when their mom took off. Kris had been angry at the world and had pushed everyone away. Kassie had stuffed down her anger and found her escape through music, which had driven an even bigger wedge between her and her father. Alyssa had gone off the deep end, setting out on a trajectory that would likely land her in prison…or dead.

Kris pulled away, blinking back tears. "Thanks. Shannon will help, too."

Kassie looked at Jared. "How could this happen with police driving by?"

"I'm sure whoever did this didn't park in the driveway. He probably left his vehicle some distance away, walked along the bayou and slipped in your back door. Most of the blinds are drawn, too. Nothing would have been obvious from the road."

Officer Bloom pocketed his camera. "Any idea who might have done this?"

Kris shook her head. "A few days ago, Kassie surprised someone on one of our boats. Then someone broke into the office. We think it was the same person."

Officer Bloom looked at Jared. "Do you know anything about this?"

"Yeah. Dave and Trey responded to the incident on the boat. I was the responding officer for the break-in at the office." He filled him in on the details.

The officer looked around him. "Someone was apparently searching for something."

Jared nodded. "At the charter office, too."

Bloom looked at Kris, then Kassie. "Any idea what he's looking for?"

Kris shook her head. "Not a clue."

Kassie pressed her lips together. Kris would be ticked, but the police needed leads. Until they figured out who was behind the attacks and what they wanted, none of them would be safe, including little Gavin.

"Our father might have been involved in something we don't know about."

Kris spun toward her, fists clenched. "That's nothing more than a wild guess."

Kassie ignored the venom in her sister's tone. "Do you have a better explanation? Like Officer Bloom said, they're looking for something. I don't have anything these guys might want. Do you?"

"Of course not."

"If you don't and I don't, that leaves Dad. Since it was his boat, his office and his house, it's a no-brainer."

Officer Bloom raised his brows. "This is your dad's house?"

Kris sighed. "It's in our mom's name, but yes, our dad lived here."

After several more questions, Bloom tucked his notepad into his shirt pocket. "I'll see if I can lift prints."

Jared nodded. "The guy on the boat wore gloves, and we weren't able to get any identifiable prints at the office, but it's worth a shot."

Kassie looked around at the mess. "I don't know where you'd begin." The odds of getting anything useful were almost nil. Having to clean up messy black powder on top of everything else would probably send Kris into meltdown mode.

"Let me at least get the door where he came in."

Kris agreed, and Bloom stepped out to retrieve his kit. A few minutes later, he was finished.

"That's it. If we need anything else, we'll let you know."

As Jared walked him out, Kassie turned to Kris, jaw set. "You can't stay here."

"Where would we go?"

"You can stay with me."

"Gavin, Bella and me, all piling in on you." Skepticism filled her tone.

Kassie winced. Her three-bedroom home overlooking the park in the North Hill Historic District suited her fine, but it was a fraction of the size of the family home. These days,

even that wouldn't be big enough to alleviate the friction between them.

Kris cast a glance at the clock. "Shannon will be off work
in ten minutes. I'll give her a call."

Jared stepped back into the room, and Kassie continued.
"If Shannon can't put you guys up, you need to stay with me.
Y'all shouldn't be here alone."

When Jared agreed, Kris nodded. "All right."

Jared's gaze shifted back and forth between the two of
them. "You both worked in your dad's business, right?"

Kassie shrugged. "To some degree."

"And neither of you have any idea who these guys are or
what they're looking for?"

Kassie studied him. Was that doubt in his features?

He continued. "First the boat, then the office, then the
house. Someone's awfully determined to find something. They
may not quit until they get what they're looking for. Once
we identify the *something*, it might lead us to the *someone*.
If either of you know anything, you'd better speak up before
someone gets hurt."

Kris crossed her arms and glared at Jared. Kassie felt some
of that indignation herself. The man was accusing them of
withholding information.

She pushed aside her irritation. She'd had the same doubts,
wondering if Kris was covering for their dad. Jared was a cop.
It was his job to ask the difficult questions.

Kris apparently didn't see it that way. She uncrossed her
arms and stepped closer, her anger directed fully at Kassie.
"You and Dad never got along. Now, instead of finally letting go of the animosity you have toward him, you're trashing
his reputation when he's no longer here to defend himself."

Gavin began to cry at his mother's outburst and slid a thumb
into his mouth. Before Kassie or Kris could disentangle them-

selves from their toe-to-toe encounter, Jared knelt in front of Gavin and held out both hands. "It's okay, buddy. Come here."

The little boy cast a glance back at his mother and aunt. After another moment of hesitation, he flung himself into Jared's arms. Kassie's surprise instantly morphed to guilt. Maybe Gavin sought solace from a virtual stranger because that stranger was the only calm person in the room.

Kris was right on one account—she *was* having a hard time letting go of her animosity. It wasn't that she hadn't tried. She was well-acquainted with the Bible's commands to forgive, to make things right with those who'd wronged her. That was hard to do when someone was dead.

But her suspicions about her father had nothing to do with whatever resentment she might be feeling. Before she could say so, the jangle of the house phone cut her off. Kris stalked to the desk in the corner and picked up the receiver. After her initial "Hello," her responses were clipped.

Kassie cast a glance at Jared, who was still holding Gavin. The boy's arms were wrapped around him, his head nestled into the crook of Jared's neck. Kassie sighed. Ms. MaryAnn probably hadn't told him about her dysfunctional family. If he was expecting the faultless woman his grandmother had described, the real Kassie would be quite a disappointment.

She shook off the thought. Regardless of Ms. MaryAnn's hopes, she and Jared weren't headed toward any kind of romance. Even without her reluctance to risk repeating past mistakes, she had too much on her plate to consider a serious relationship. So why did she care so much about what Jared thought of her?

Kris brushed off her caller with an "I'm not interested" and hung up the phone. As she walked away from the desk, she threw up her hands. "I have no patience for sales calls this afternoon. Besides, the connection was stinky."

Jared frowned. "Stinky in what way?"

"Like static, with a soft hum in between."

He put Gavin down and strode toward the phone. "Get me a screwdriver." A minute later, he had the insides of the receiver exposed. "There's a wiretap here."

Kris's jaw dropped. "We have a bug?"

"You do. If the intruder put it here today, he might have put one on the office phone last night, too."

Kassie sank onto the living room couch, and Gavin crawled up next to her. She'd called Kris from the office phone last night. If the intruders were listening, they'd have known about her plans to visit Kris, right down to the time she'd arrive. Trailing her would have been easy.

She turned toward Jared, eyes wide. "I led them here."

Jared sank down next to her and put an encouraging hand on her shoulder. "Not necessarily. If someone wanted to find this place, they'd only have to search for the name on the property appraiser's website."

Kassie shook her head. "The deed is under Singleton, our mother's maiden name. The Ashbaugh name isn't on there anywhere. No, I led them here."

Kris pulled her cell phone from her purse. Her anger seemed to have dissipated. "I'll call Shannon."

Two minutes later, she disconnected the call. "I can stay with her. She says it'll be fun."

"Good." Jared rose and walked toward the door. "I have to report for my shift in less than an hour. I'll wait outside while you get your things together and make sure you're not followed."

Kris jogged toward the stairs. "I'll be right down."

Kassie watched her disappear, then wrapped an arm around Gavin. Bella lay at her feet.

She should be hurt that Kris would turn first to Shannon, unwilling to accept Kassie's help except as a last resort. Sisters—

especially twins—should be like best friends. Healthy families relied on each other and stuck together through thick and thin.

But no one would characterize the relationships in the Ashbaugh family as healthy. No matter how Kassie wished otherwise, she and Kris and Alyssa would never share the closeness that some of the siblings she knew had. That was especially obvious tonight.

Because as her sister was upstairs packing to take her son and dog to her best friend's house, Kassie didn't feel pain or sadness or even disappointment.

Instead, she felt relief.

FIVE

Kassie slouched over her dad's desk and put her face in her hands. Papers were scattered in front of her, incomplete spreadsheets filled with chicken scratch. Kris had said their dad had handled the accounting for the past eight years. This wasn't accounting. More like sporadic notes, numbers jotted here and there—nothing that made sense. Maybe she should start with the bank accounts. At least everything that went in or out would be recorded.

A soft knock on the doorjamb pulled her away from her accounting woes. Kris stood in the open doorway. "I have to pick up Gavin from the babysitter in twenty minutes. Are you ready to leave?"

Five days had passed since the break-in at Kris's house. The brief reprieve hadn't lulled Kassie into a state of complacency. Just the opposite. Rather than giving up, the intruder had probably been looking for the ideal time to strike. The situation had left her with an ever-present tension, that itchy sensation of being watched.

The investigation wasn't going anywhere, either. The prints lifted at Kris's had led nowhere. With the lack of witnesses and the intruder's knack for leaving no evidence, the authorities were no closer to figuring out who was behind the break-ins than they'd been the day Kassie was attacked on the boat.

She shuffled the papers into a haphazard stack. "I suppose."

If she defined *ready* as the sense of accomplishment that came with getting a lot done, she wasn't ready. *Ready* wouldn't happen anytime soon.

She rose and followed Kris to the front, hitting lights on her way through. The two of them, along with Shannon, had spent a three-hour block of time two separate afternoons getting the house back in order. They were close enough to being finished that Kris had insisted she and Shannon would take care of the rest. They'd also agreed neither of them would work at the office alone. When Kris hadn't been available, Buck had shown up.

Kris cast her a glance over one shoulder. "How are you coming with the books?"

"Slow. Dad might have been a good charter captain, but he made a horrible accountant." She struggled to keep the annoyance from her tone. No sense in starting another argument.

Kris shrugged. "I guess that wasn't his strong suit, but he was trying to save money."

Kassie slid the key into the lock. Her dad's decision to handle the bookkeeping himself likely had nothing to do with saving money. That was another thought she'd keep to herself.

As she turned from the locked door, her ringtone sounded from inside her purse. She pulled out her phone and groaned. "It's Alyssa."

Kris smiled. "Better you than me."

Kassie put the phone to her ear. Since Kris was the last one to talk to her, it was Kassie's turn. Kris got into her car, and Kassie waved her on. At five in the afternoon, plenty of people were out and about. She gave Kris a second wave as she passed, then continued walking toward the Sorento a few spots down. Parking in the area consisted of spaces end to end, lining both sides of the street, plus a small lot at the corner.

Alyssa's voice came through the phone. "How are you?"

It was how she started every conversation, the inquiry into

their welfare, as if she cared. Since neither Kassie nor Kris had spoken with her since Kris told her about their father's disappearance, she knew nothing about the events of last week. But now, alone on the roadside, it wasn't the time to fill her in.

"Just busy keeping Kassie's Kuts going while handling the charter business."

"How's that going? You're getting Dad's affairs handled?"

"Working on it. It's just a long process." She could guess where the conversation was headed. Alyssa wanted to know what was in it for her.

"What are you going to do with the business?"

"We need to sell it, but I'm not ready to fight that battle with Kris yet."

"What about the house?"

"Kris and Gavin are still living there. For the time being, that'll continue."

"You do realize I'm entitled to one-third of everything."

Yep. Alyssa was never known for subtlety, especially when she wanted something.

"We're each entitled to one-third, but that won't happen until the legal stuff is wrapped up. It could take months, if not years. You'll get your share."

A frustrated sigh came through the phone. Alyssa wasn't known for patience, either. Or empathy. All her life, she'd looked out for number one. "How about if y'all buy me out?"

"Neither of us have that kind of cash, and there's not that much in the business, either. Besides, we don't know the value of everything."

"Just give me $10,000 to start, and we can settle up later. My car's on its last legs."

Kassie pressed the key fob and a beep accompanied the click of the SUV's locks. Alyssa was staying true to form. The only time she ever called was when she needed money.

"Look, Alyssa, I've got too much on my plate to deal with

your problems. Besides sorting through the business stuff, we've had break-ins at the office and house. So you'll have to solve this one on your own."

She dropped the phone into her purse and stepped from the sidewalk to cross between her SUV and the vehicle behind it. As she reached the left end of her bumper, advancing footsteps drew her attention, and she cast a glance over her shoulder. The man from the charter barreled toward her. A split second later, he slammed into her, pinning her against the back of her vehicle.

She looked frantically side to side. No one was walking down the sidewalk. The light at the corner was red, stopping traffic proceeding toward her. No vehicles were passing from behind her, either. There was no one to help her.

"What do you want?" She tried to keep the fear out of her tone but wasn't successful.

"You know what I want." Without warning, he snatched her purse from her shoulder and threw her into the street. Pain shot through her arm. At the loud squeal of tires, she rolled toward her vehicle. A pickup truck lurched to a stop, inches from where she lay.

The driver jumped out and circled his truck. "Are you all right?"

"I'm not sure." She pushed herself to a seated position. Her left shoulder throbbed. Her elbow did, too. She straightened and flexed her arm. Nothing seemed to be broken.

He extended a hand. "Can I help you get up?"

"Thanks."

She picked up her keys from where they'd landed on the pavement. After he helped her to her feet, she leaned against the back bumper. A watery weakness had settled in her limbs.

The man had taken her purse. Had he thrown her into the street to keep her from chasing him?

Or had he intended to kill her?

* * *

Jared glanced in his rearview mirror at the brown-and-black face framed there. "Are you ready to go to work, boy?"

The dog responded with an enthusiastic bark.

Work was another word he understood, like *boat*. Both seemed to excite him equally. One characteristic his dog possessed in spades was enthusiasm. Whether chasing down bad guys or sitting on the cushioned seat of the MasterCraft, the wind in his face, Justice seemed to view every activity as an opportunity for fun.

"I'll try to keep you busy tonight." Currently, he was on his way to the station. His shift wouldn't start for another twenty minutes.

He'd checked in with Sam this morning to see if there'd been any progress on IDing the guy behind the break-ins. His friend had come up with a few possibilities but had eliminated them upon learning those suspects were either currently incarcerated or dead. He was still checking leads, though, and had promised to report back soon.

Jared had also run Kassie's father's information through the database. Other than a couple of speeding tickets, his record was clean.

A block from the station, his radio crackled to life and the dispatcher's voice filled the car. It wasn't even dark yet, and some poor woman had had her purse snatched. When the dispatcher gave the location, his chest tightened. The attack had happened one building down from Ashbaugh Charters.

He drew in a stabilizing breath. The odds that Kassie was involved were slim to none. It was probably someone walking down the sidewalk, a woman who'd just stepped out of one of the neighboring businesses. Or even someone headed into the Seville Quarter for some nighttime entertainment.

Two units radioed that they were en route. Instead of pulling into the station, Jared drove past and took the next right. He was five minutes away. He'd drive by and make sure it wasn't Kassie who'd been attacked before reporting for his shift.

When he turned onto Government Street, flashing blue lights lit up the area just ahead. Police cruisers occupied parking spaces, one on each side of the street. Jared slowed to a crawl and glanced left. A Chevy pickup was parked there, Kassie's Sorento behind it. A man stood beside the truck, talking with a police officer. A woman stood nearby, facing the building. A dark ponytail hung halfway down her back.

Jared's pulse kicked into high gear. That wasn't necessarily Kassie. But he had to check. As he pulled into the empty spot behind one of the cruisers, the officer killed his lights and eased into traffic. The woman turned, her gaze following the path of the officer. It was Kassie.

His heart lurched. He'd seen her only once in the past few days. Gram had sent him out to get the mail, and Kassie had just pulled in. He'd walked over to see how she was and they'd ended up talking for twenty minutes. She'd been doing well, no new scares. Apparently, that reprieve had ended.

As he stepped from the car, Justice watched, body rigid with excitement.

"All right. You can come."

After letting the dog exit the passenger side, he crossed the street and approached the three standing on the sidewalk. Kassie gave him the briefest glance before zeroing in on his dog.

"Justice! How's my baby boy?" She cupped the dog's cheeks with both hands, then straightened. Only then did she greet Jared.

He looked her up and down. She didn't have any visible injuries. Some of his tension slipped away.

He lifted a brow. "You're the one who called the police?"

"Yeah. Actually, this gentleman did." She tilted her head toward the man still talking with the police officer.

Both of the men made eye contact with Jared. He knew the officer—Rick Danforth. He'd worked with him for the past two years.

He returned Danforth's greeting with a friendly one of his own. "Anything I can do?"

Although he'd directed his question to his fellow officer, it was Kassie who answered.

"See if Justice can find my purse."

Upon hearing his name, the dog's tail wagged even harder. He nudged Kassie's hand with his nose. Jared frowned. What was up with his dog?

"We can look, but don't get your hopes up. He's great at what he does, but he's not Bella."

Danforth lifted his brows. "You two know each other?"

Jared nodded. "We're neighbors. What happened? Not to cut in on your investigation or anything."

"No problem. I guess you heard the call. The lady was leaving the charter company, walking to her car. Some guy barreled into her, snatched her purse and threw her into the road."

Jared looked at the other man. "Did you witness it?"

"I did. The creep threw her right in front of my truck." He tipped his head toward the Chevy next to them.

Kassie looked at the man with appreciation in her gaze. "If it weren't for your quick reflexes, I might have been a hood ornament. Or a pancake."

"If you wouldn't have acted so fast and rolled, my quick reflexes wouldn't have done you much good."

Kassie looked up at Jared. "I recognized him. No mask this time. It was the charter customer."

The man he saw leaving the marina. "Which way did he go?"

The pickup driver pointed ahead. "He ran that way, shot across the road and made a left on Tarragona Street. He had her purse when I lost sight of him. I hated to let him get away, but no way was I going to leave her lying on the pavement."

Danforth picked up the conversation. "Warren responded the same time I did. He's looking for anyone who matches the description Ms. Ashbaugh gave, but it's a long shot. If the guy got into a car, he's gone."

Jared nodded. "I'll head that direction and see if we notice anything."

Not likely. But he'd at least check. Sometimes it was insignificant things that solved cases—pieces of evidence dropped and left behind near crime scenes.

He met Danforth's gaze. "If I'm not back when you finish, can you make sure she gets away okay?"

"Sure thing."

As Jared crossed the street, Justice cast several glances over his shoulder. The dog was probably seeing if Kassie would follow. Jared shook his head. If Justice started acting that way with everybody, he'd question the dog's fitness for police work.

When they got to the corner, he headed down the sidewalk at a slow jog, paralleling Tarragona Street. A short distance away, a trash container sat next to a building, its plastic lid thrown back. Justice slowed. No way was someone hiding in there.

The dog stopped and whined, looking back over his shoulder. Jared moved closer to the dumpster to peer over its edge. Several bulging plastic bags had been tossed inside, a brown leather handbag lying on top.

The color and style were similar to what he'd seen Kassie carry, but he was no expert on ladies' fashions. He reached in and looped a finger over the shoulder strap to slide the object closer. Once he'd lifted it out, he used a discarded napkin to fold back the flap and remove the wallet. Soon, Kassie's face stared back at him from the driver's license tucked behind the clear protector.

He looked at his dog, jaw slack. "Good boy, Justice."

When he got back to where he'd left Kassie and Danforth, the officer was watching her get into her Sorento. Jared held up his arm, her purse dangling by its strap.

She stepped from her SUV, a smile spreading across her face and lighting up her vibrant blue eyes. He liked being the cause of one of those smiles.

She hurried toward him. "I don't suppose Justice tackled somebody to get this."

"'Fraid not. But he did hesitate at the dumpster it had been tossed into."

She bent to wrap her arms around the dog's neck. "Good boy. You found Kassie's purse." She nuzzled the top of his head with her chin. "You're not just a pretty boy. You're smart, too."

When she reached for the object, Jared stopped her. "Let's try to lift prints first."

"I've got it." Danforth motioned them toward his cruiser. Using the hood as a working surface, he was able to lift four viable prints. They were probably Kassie's, but maybe they'd get a break.

"When the guy had me pinned against my car, I asked him what he wanted, and he said that I know what he wants." She paused, eyebrows drawn together. "I don't. If I had any clue, I'd gladly give him whatever he wants, just to make this stop."

Jared's heart twisted. "We're doing everything we can." Unfortunately, the suspect wasn't giving them anything to work with.

When Danforth had finished, he handed the purse to Kassie. "See if anything is missing."

She removed her wallet and thumbed through its contents. "My money and credit cards are untouched."

She fished through the rest of the items, her movements becoming more frantic. "My phone is gone."

Jared stepped closer. "You're sure you didn't leave it in the charter office or in your car?"

"I'm positive. Alyssa called as I was walking out. My younger sister." She paused, catching herself in the middle of an eye roll. "Anyway, when I got to my car, I hung up and dropped my phone into my purse. The guy was watching me. He wanted my phone."

Jared had to agree. He just couldn't guess why.

The man hadn't been able to find what he was looking for on the boat, in the charter office or in the house.

What could he possibly hope to find on Kassie's phone?

SIX

Kassie rose from the old piano, letting one hand slide lightly over the keys. It had become part of the Ashbaugh home twenty years ago, and Kassie had had her first lesson a week later. With the exception of the four years she was away at school, she'd taken it with her everywhere she'd lived.

Currently, a book of classical favorites sat against the music rack, open to Beethoven's "Moonlight Sonata." No matter how crazy life got, she tried to make time at least a couple days a week to play. It was how she unwound from the daily stress.

This afternoon, she needed that stress relief. While Buck had handled a small morning charter, she'd again tackled the job of trying to construct some accounting records. It was going to take forever to put together what she'd need to list the business for sale. It would take longer than forever to convince Kris that selling the business was the right decision.

She stepped to the wall to close the window, then did the same in the kitchen and dining room. With highs in the mid-seventies, it was perfect open-window weather, a chance to air out the house and bring the freshness inside. Soon she'd have to run the AC. Once May arrived, Pensacola would begin its trek toward the hot mugginess of summer.

After closing all the windows, she snatched her purse from where she'd hung it over one of the dining room chairs and headed toward the front door. Her biweekly Saturday game night with Ms. MaryAnn was another stress reliever. She didn't even have to make dinner. Ms. MaryAnn always insisted.

Today, Kassie had insisted. Ms. MaryAnn didn't need to spend an hour on her feet preparing dinner a week after finishing rehab for a broken hip. Kassie had lost the argument, because Jared's insistence had been even more vehement. She was entertaining his grandma so he was providing dinner. She'd be expecting DoorDash from one of the local restaurants, except Ms. MaryAnn had already told her Jared was a great cook during one of her *you've-got-to-meet-my-amazing-grandson* sales pitches.

After locking the front door, Kassie stepped off the porch with a sudden lightness in her chest. She squared her shoulders. Her anticipation had nothing to do with the thought of spending the evening with Jared. She'd always been a game buff. Seeing Justice again would be fun, too.

Tomorrow, Bella would be joining her, along with Kris and Gavin. The three of them had come over yesterday evening to celebrate Gavin's birthday, and Kris had asked about staying with her. It would just be temporary, she'd promised, to give Shannon and her boyfriend a break. He was over often and didn't seem to like the company when he was. Kris's new living arrangements weren't working out as well as she'd hoped.

A half minute after Kassie rang the bell, the door swung inward to reveal a smiling Jared, wearing jeans and a "Dog Dad" T-shirt. Since she wasn't supposed to notice how well he filled out said T-shirt, she dragged her gaze from him to Justice. The dog's tail wagged furiously, and he released an excited bark.

Kassie scratched his head and cheeks. "I still say he seems too friendly to be a police dog."

"He's not ferocious unless warranted. But he's usually not this friendly. You have a weird effect on him."

She straightened and smiled. "I guess that's a good thing."

"As long as I don't ever have to apprehend you."

"Since I don't plan to get on the wrong side of the law, that shouldn't be a problem." She drew in a deep breath. "Dinner smells good."

"I hope it tastes as good as it smells."

"If you're half the cook your grandma says you are, it'll be to die for."

"Grandma tends to exaggerate."

She grinned. "I got that impression."

She'd probably been the subject of some of that exaggeration herself. Living up to it all would be impossible.

She followed him toward the kitchen. "Can I help you finish up?"

"I've got it. You can relax and visit with Gram."

When Kassie reached the combination kitchen/dining room, Ms. MaryAnn was seated in one of the captain's chairs, her walker next to her.

"Welcome, sweetheart. Jared will have dinner ready shortly. The chicken has another seven minutes."

"It smells wonderful."

"I told you he was a good cook."

Kassie grinned at him, and he rolled his eyes. At least, he had started to when his grandma looked in his direction. He froze and cleared his throat.

"Don't you roll your eyes at me, young man. I'm not saying anything that isn't true."

"Yes, ma'am." His tone was serious, but a grin quivered at the corners of his mouth.

Kassie headed toward one of the cabinets. "I'll set the table."

She knew her way around Ms. MaryAnn's kitchen. Though the elderly woman always insisted on cooking, she let Kassie wash and put away the dishes.

While she set the table, Jared fed Justice. Soon, the three of them were seated, the whole spread laid out in front of them.

Kassie eyed the dish of scalloped potatoes, bowl of steamed broccoli and platter of baked chicken. "You went all out."

Jared shrugged. "I like to eat."

Ms. MaryAnn patted her wrist. "Don't let him fool you. He likes to cook, too."

Jared offered a prayer of thanks for the meal, ending with a request to protect Kassie.

She looked at Jared. "Anything exciting happen last night?"

"Nothing out of the ordinary. A domestic disturbance, a guy who'd had too much to drink." He frowned. "A purse-snatching."

Kassie cast a sideways glance at Ms. MaryAnn, who'd just taken a bite of chicken. Did she know? The way Jared had ended his prayer, he wasn't keeping everything from her.

Kassie returned her gaze to Jared. "Any breaks on the purse-snatching?"

"Not yet. We've tried to have the phone pinged but nothing. Either it's been destroyed or it's being protected by signal-blocking technology, like a Faraday bag."

She'd learned that from Officer Danforth this afternoon, then bought a new phone and imported her contacts and other info. She'd kept the same number since it was the after-hours one for the salon and the charter company.

Ms. MaryAnn took a big swig of tea. "I was horrified when Jared told me. I'm so glad you weren't hurt."

"Me, too." Her arm was sore from landing on it, but it could have been a lot worse. Especially if that truck had hit her. "I got my purse back, just not my phone."

Jared frowned. "You might have to replace it."

"I already have." She needed a phone too badly to go without one for long.

"Also, that car we saw at Ever'Man was a rental secured with the same fake ID presented to Ashbaugh Charters."

"So we're back to square one."

Ms. MaryAnn broke the brief silence that followed. "By the way, we enjoyed the concert this afternoon."

Good, some lighter conversation. "You went to a concert?"

"Nope, didn't have to leave the house. Jared made me turn off the TV so he could listen."

When Kassie finally caught on, heat crept up her cheeks. The last half hour, her playing had produced what she hoped were some pleasant sounds, but she'd started off her practice session learning something new. If she'd known she had an audience, she'd have only played what she was proficient at.

Jared smiled. "I enjoyed it. I appreciate the work involved in learning to play like that."

"Do you play?"

"Not piano. I played trumpet in junior high and high school. Kind of let it go when I wasn't in band anymore."

"Through my teen years, I was constantly at the piano. My mom was a good flutist, and we played a lot together. As an adult, I haven't stayed with it like I wish I had." In fact, there'd been periods of time when she went weeks without playing. Musical skill wasn't always appreciated in apartment settings. Or by people who resented anything that took the focus off themselves.

When all three plates were empty, Jared pushed his chair back from the table. "Are you ladies ready for peach cobbler?"

Kassie groaned. "I'm full, but I can always make room for dessert."

While she cleared the table, Jared dished up the cobbler, then spooned a mountain of whipped cream over each serving. Since it came out of one of his grandmother's metal mixing bowls, he'd likely made it from scratch.

When she returned to her chair, Justice approached. His eyes seemed to hold sadness. Or longing.

"What's the matter, baby? Is no one paying attention to you?" She scratched the back of his neck with both hands, working her way around the sides to his throat. His tail moved back and forth, and he lowered his head to rest it in her lap.

Jared cleared his throat. "What have you done to my dog?"

"I think he likes me."

"That's an understatement."

When they finished dessert, she had to lift the dog's head off her lap to stand. She put the leftovers into plastic containers while Jared washed the dishes. Soon she was ready for game night.

She looked at Jared. "Are you going to play with us?"

"I'll pass. Like most grandmas, mine thinks the sun rises and sets on me, but you don't want to see me play Boggle, or any word game, for that matter."

"You can't be that bad."

"Yeah, I can. I was diagnosed with mild dyslexia as a child, and my spelling is still pretty bad. Thank the Lord we do reports on computer now instead of having to handwrite them."

He walked from the room. When his dog didn't follow, he patted his thigh. "Come on, boy. Let's go out."

After three four-minute rounds, words filled Kassie's sheet of paper. MaryAnn's list was comparable. The front door opened and closed again. Both man and dog remained outside of her view, but judging from Jared's laughter and Justice's playful growls, they were wrestling on the living room floor.

The next several rounds, Kassie tried to block out the activity. One look at the scores showed the success of that endeavor. Ms. MaryAnn was killing her.

Jared's playfulness and affection for his dog stirred something in her, and an unexpected sense of loneliness swept through her. She needed to get a dog. That was all. She certainly didn't need a man.

"You seem distracted." Ms. MaryAnn's words sliced across her thoughts, drawing her attention back to the game. "Or maybe I should say you look contemplative."

"I was thinking about adopting a dog." Not seriously, but since the thought had crossed her mind, the statement was true.

"You were?"

"Dogs are great company. When you're a dog mom, you get undying love and devotion. In a dog's eyes, you're perfect. There's no such thing as mistakes or faults or shortcomings."

"Sounds like you've had those pointed out a few too many times."

Ms. MaryAnn was too perceptive.

"A few." Like every day of her life growing up. And too many times as an adult.

The guys she'd dated hadn't understood her drive. Most had lost interest after a couple of months. Except the last one. Instead of bailing, Paul had made her his project, thinking he could change her to fit his image of the perfect mate. When gentle manipulation hadn't worked, he'd resorted to insults and harsh criticism. As a child, she'd had to take it. As an adult, she didn't and finally kicked him to the curb. Unfortunately, some barbs sank in more deeply than others and were much harder to extract.

Ms. MaryAnn gave her a sympathetic smile. "There *are* good men out there." The older woman's gaze shifted toward the living room, silently pointing out one of those good men. Kassie had no doubt Jared was one. But between running her salon and keeping Ashbaugh Charters afloat, all while navigating the minefield of Kris's feelings, she was too overloaded to even think about romance.

Besides that, regardless of his grandmother's matchmaking attempts, Jared hadn't shown that kind of interest in her, just neighborly concern and a desire for justice that any good cop would feel. Maybe he didn't even find her attractive. Maybe he preferred tall model types over women who couldn't access the top shelves of their kitchen cabinets without a stool.

When they'd completed their usual ten rounds, Ms. Mary-

Ann had finished twenty points in the lead. She pushed herself up from the table and retrieved her walker. "Good game, even if you were distracted." She gave her a wink.

Great. She was soon to be the subject of yet another conversation. When she stepped into the living room, Jared rose from the couch. "Justice and I will walk you home."

"Sounds good." She'd never worried about it before. Tonight she was glad for the company, both human and canine.

She walked across the yard, Jared next to her, Justice trailing behind, and then stepped onto her porch. "Thank you for dinner. It was really good."

"We'll do it again soon."

When she slid her key into the lock, Justice whined.

She turned back around. "It's okay, boy. You'll see me again."

Jared's eyes widened almost imperceptibly, and his jaw went slack. Kassie waited, but he didn't share the revelation.

After stepping inside and saying goodnight to Jared and his dog, she closed and relocked the door.

Thirty minutes later, she was propped up in bed with her reader. When her new cell phone rang from its place on the nightstand, she frowned at it. Who would be calling her at ten thirty at night?

She glanced at the screen and heaved a sigh. Alyssa. She could ignore it, but Alyssa would keep calling. Might as well get it over with.

She swiped the phone and gave a terse "Hello."

"I've been trying to call you since Tuesday night. It wouldn't go through."

"My phone was stolen. I just got a new one this afternoon." She paused. "If this is about your inheritance, nothing has changed since we last talked."

Alyssa made a sound of annoyance. "You and Kris always assume the worst about me."

"That's because you usually fulfill our expectations." She winced. That wasn't the Christian thing to say. "I'm sorry. What did you need?"

"I had a strange phone call. Shortly after we hung up Tuesday night, someone called me, said they were a friend of Dad's and wanted to know where he was. I told them he fell overboard and drowned."

Kassie's pulse picked up. The man who stole her phone. Alyssa was at the top of her recent calls. He probably hadn't been close enough to overhear her conversation, but he wouldn't have had to read many texts to gather that they were sisters.

"Anyhow, the guy said he believes Dad is alive and hiding. He said he has ways of drawing him out."

Kassie's heart pounded in her ears. "What did you say?"

"I told him if anyone would know where he was, it would be my sister."

Now Kassie did groan. "Are you crazy?"

"Why? What's wrong?"

Kassie drew in a breath. All Alyssa knew, beyond a casual mention of break-ins, was that their father had disappeared. No one had filled her in on the details or about Tuesday's attack.

"I'm sorry." Second apology in a matter of minutes. She wasn't doing very well. Of course, conversations with Alyssa rarely went well. "Someone ransacked the Cabo, the charter office and Kris's house. Tuesday night I was attacked. Someone is determined to get their hands on something."

There was a long pause before Alyssa responded. "If you didn't always keep me on the outside of everything, I'd have known these things and handled that call differently."

Kassie tamped down a defensive retort. "It's okay. You didn't know the full story."

After finishing the call, she put the phone back on the nightstand. Soon the tablet joined it. No way could she focus on reading now. Sleep was probably out of the question, too.

The sister Alyssa mentioned would be Kris—the favorite daughter, the athletic one who enjoyed fishing and sports, both as a participant and a spectator, the one who regularly made the meals he loved, the one for whom his smiles had always held love and approval. Not the musical one who usually had her head buried in a book and who never touched a bat or ball unless a grade depended on it, the one for whom his gaze had held disappointment.

She lay back and closed her eyes, determined to slow her thoughts and get some sleep. When that didn't work, she rose from the bed to trudge to the kitchen. Maybe a cup of chamomile tea would do the trick.

After putting the mug of water into the microwave, she leaned back against the counter to wait for it to heat. Tomorrow she would talk to Jared. Maybe this newest development was cause for additional concern. Or maybe the whole thing came out of Alyssa's imagination. She'd always been one for drama, however she could create it.

At the beep of the microwave, she removed the mug and dropped a tea bag into the steaming water. As she set the mug on the kitchen table, a subtle sound came from a few feet away. She spun toward the back door, every muscle drawn taut. With the back porch light off, nothing was visible through the nine rectangular panes of glass except darkness.

The back door exploded inward with the sharp crack of splitting wood. She screamed and ran toward the hallway, the blare of the alarm surrounding her. She'd barely made it from the kitchen when one thick arm wrapped around her waist and a hand clamped over her mouth and nose. Her assailant hiked the arm that held her higher, and her feet left the floor.

As he dragged her back into the kitchen and toward the door, she struggled against him, kicking and trying to pry his hand from her mouth. He only tightened his hold, his hand cupped just enough that she couldn't sink her teeth into it. Her bare heels against his shins accomplished nothing. She looked frantically around the kitchen for anything she could use as a weapon. The cast-iron skillet she used to make her eggs sat in its usual spot on the stove. It wasn't large, but it was hard and thick. It was also far out of her reach. But the tea...

As he passed the table, she snatched the mug, sloshing some of the steeping tea onto her hand. Then she tipped her head to the side and tossed the rest over her shoulder. A bellow near her ear told her that the steaming liquid had hit its mark. The hold on her briefly loosened, and she twisted away from him. The mug fell to the floor with the crash of shattering porcelain. A second later, she wrapped her hand around the skillet's handle and spun. It connected against the side of his head with a solid *thunk*.

He staggered sideways, and one hand went behind him. When he brought it back out, he was holding a black object. A flick of his wrist exposed a lethal-looking blade.

For several tense moments, they stood staring at one another, him holding the knife, her clutching the cast-iron skillet. Her breath came in jagged gasps, and the alarm continued to blare, shredding her already frayed nerves.

Suddenly, he spun and darted out the door.

Kassie stood motionless for several more moments. Then her knees buckled, and she collapsed to the tile floor in a crumpled heap.

SEVEN

Jared moaned and pulled the spare pillow over his ear. The alarm was already going off, and it seemed as if he'd just fallen asleep. Justice was barking too. What was wrong with his dog? The alarm never bothered him.

He opened one eye. The red numerals on his digital alarm clock glowed in the dark room—12:17. *What?*

The confusion fled his brain in an instant. That was a house alarm, and it sounded as if it was coming from right next door. He jumped from the bed, grabbing his cell phone and keys in one hand and weapon in the other. "Come on, Justice. Let's go."

He hit the front door at a half-run and threw both locks, Justice right on his heels. The squeal of the alarm was definitely coming from next door. After locking Gram inside, he jumped from the porch and ran toward Kassie's house. The front door was shut, and no windows appeared broken.

As he rounded the corner into her back yard, a shadowed figure had almost reached the fence separating Kassie's back yard from the one behind it.

He raised the weapon. "Stop! Police."

The suspect's head swiveled, but he didn't slow his retreat. Jared pointed that direction. "Go, Justice. Take him down."

The dog bounded forward, legs a blur in the light of a half-moon. Jared glanced back at Kassie's house. The patio light was on. A gaping hole occupied the space where the door was supposed to be. His steps faltered, but his hesitation lasted only a moment. The alarm system would have called 911. With the would-be intruder fleeing, Kassie was no longer in imminent danger.

Unless the man had hurt her.

Indecision gripped him again, as brief as before. No, if he could ask Kassie, she would tell him to follow his dog and try to catch the guy while he had the opportunity.

He took off after Justice, his bare feet muffled against the carpet of grass. The man had climbed the fence and disappeared into the next yard.

Justice cleared the obstruction with little effort, and Jared followed. Ahead of them, a car waited at the edge of the road just out of the circle of light cast by a nearby streetlamp. If that was where the guy was headed, Justice would reach him before he could get the door open.

"Hurry, boy." He spoke the words under his breath. Justice knew what to do, had done it dozens of times. He just had to reach the guy before the guy got to the car.

Suddenly, the vehicle's back door swung open and the suspect dove into the seat headfirst. The car took off, tires squealing against the asphalt. Justice's powerful jaws snapped closed over the space where the guy's ankle had been a fraction of a second earlier.

"Justice, heel." As badly as Jared wanted to put an end to this, he couldn't risk the safety of his dog.

The vehicle passed under the streetlight, and the man in the back sat up and closed the door. The car held two occupants, but Jared couldn't make out either of them.

He waved a hand. "Come on, boy. Let's check on Kassie."

Justice fell in next to him as he jogged toward the house. Distant sirens assured him the police would be there shortly.

Lights had come on in two of the neighboring houses, with one man venturing outside.

As he approached Kassie's, the squeal of her alarm grew louder. When he stepped into her kitchen, the back door wasn't missing as he'd initially thought. It was slammed back against the wall, hanging crooked from one hinge. Some kind of liquid, likely tea, had been splashed on the floor, based on the pieces of porcelain scattered about and the curved handle of a mug still intact. A cast-iron skillet lay in the middle of the mess.

"Kassie, are you all right?"

A door creaked open in the back. "Jared?"

He moved in that direction. "Yeah, it's me. And Justice."

When he stepped into the living room, Kassie was hurrying down the hall toward them. Her hair was down, a thick mass of soft curls falling over her shoulders, deep ebony against the pale pink of the robe. She stopped and looked up at him with fear-filled eyes, and for a moment she seemed ready to throw herself into his arms.

He wouldn't have minded. She was scared half out of her mind. An unexpected longing to be the one to comfort her rose up inside.

Instead, she dropped to her knees and wrapped her arms around Justice, leaving Jared's arms feeling oddly empty. As she pressed her face against the dog's back, he stood still, letting her cling to him. Then he craned his neck to rest his muzzle against her shoulder. The sirens rose in volume and abruptly died.

When Kassie finally rose, her eyes glistened with unshed tears.

She moved past him toward the living room. "I guess I can shut this off now." She punched four numbers into the alarm's keypad, and the room fell silent. "I didn't bother before, just ran straight to my room and locked the door."

She sank onto the couch. "Did you see anything?"

"Someone jumped your back fence. I sent Justice after him, but the guy had a getaway car waiting. He jumped in and the driver sped off just as Justice reached them."

Five seconds earlier and the dog would have had the man on the ground. Five seconds. If only he'd woken up more quickly. Or not been asleep to begin with.

Working night shift, he tried not to mess up his body's rhythm by sleeping when everyone else did. His one exception, if he had Saturday off, was grabbing a few hours of sleep so he'd be fresh for church.

He laid his weapon on the end table and took a seat next to her. "What happened?" Judging from the mess in the kitchen, there'd been some kind of struggle.

"I couldn't sleep, so I got up to make some tea. I had it made and had just started it steeping when someone kicked in the door. He grabbed me and started dragging me in that direction." A shudder shook her shoulders. "I threw the hot tea in his face, then hit him in the head with the skillet."

He stretched out his legs and crossed them at the ankles. "You're pretty amazing."

Her gaze dipped downward, then swept back up to his face. "Where are your shoes?"

"I didn't take time to put them on. I just grabbed my phone, keys and pistol."

A heavy knock sounded on the front door. When she opened it, Officer Danforth stood on her porch. His eyes registered recognition. "You had a home invasion?"

Before she could answer, his gaze shifted sideways and settled on Jared. His eyebrows lifted, along with one side of his mouth.

Jared cleared his throat. "I heard the alarm from next door, and Justice and I ran right over."

He motioned Danforth into the living room and gave his

report as the officer took notes. When Jared finished, Kassie wasn't able to add anything beyond the altercation in the kitchen and the call from the alarm company while she'd hid in her locked bedroom.

Danforth slipped his pen and pad back into his pocket. "I suppose you can't shed any more light on who this might be."

"No, but I got an interesting call from my younger sister tonight."

"What kind of call?"

"Someone called her, wanted to know where our dad is, that they have reason to believe he's alive." She pursed her lips. "He claimed they have ways of drawing him out."

Jared frowned. "Everywhere they've broken in, they believed they were alone. But trying to get into your house while you're sleeping inside, they're getting bolder. Or more desperate."

"Maybe the guy didn't know I was home. My car is in the garage."

"You have a window in your garage. I think he would have checked that before kicking in the door."

She gave him a half smile. "I didn't say he was smart."

"True. Or maybe he knew you were home and wasn't counting on the alarm."

"I have a sticker in the window."

"He could have overlooked it or have been testing to see if there really was a system and if it was monitored."

If so, was his intent to ransack Kassie's house, searching for whatever he was determined to find? Or had he planned from the start to kidnap her and be gone before anyone was alerted? Maybe that was his way of drawing her father out. With that thought, a boulder settled in his gut.

After wishing Danforth farewell, Jared turned to Kassie. "We need to get your kitchen door secure."

"How bad is it?"

"Bad." The door might be usable, but the jamb would have to be rebuilt. "We'll need to board it up tonight. Do you have any plywood?"

"There's some in the garage. I think the prior owners used it to board windows during the last hurricane."

While he secured the door, she cleaned up the mess on the kitchen floor. When they were finished, he turned to face her at the front door. "You need to go somewhere safe."

"I can't just leave. I'm running two businesses. Granted, I'm not spending much time at my salon right now, thanks to my three dependable hairdressers, but I still have to show up occasionally."

"I'm sure you have some local friends."

Yeah, she had friends. She just hadn't been spending any time with them. She'd been so busy getting Kassie's Kuts going and still working in the charter business that the only social activities she'd continued were her biweekly game nights with Ms. MaryAnn.

Even with her recent neglect, any one of her friends would put her up, but she wouldn't consider it. "I can't put someone else in danger."

"Come stay with Gram and me. I'll sleep on the couch and give you the spare bedroom."

"Then your grandma would be in danger."

"I'll be there to watch you both. You shouldn't be without protection."

"You can't stay awake 24/7 and do your job." She pressed her lips together. "I'll try to come up with something."

He crossed his arms. There had to be a better solution than his leaving her alone at her home. But he couldn't force her to come with him. He'd just have to watch out for her the best he could.

When he slipped back into his grandmother's house, she was waiting for him in the living room.

"I assume that was Kassie's alarm I heard. Is everything okay?"

"Now it is. Someone broke in, possibly even tried to abduct her."

Her eyes widened. "Oh, no! She needs to stay here."

He held both hands out to the side. "I tried. She doesn't want to put you in danger."

"You at least have her house secure, right?"

"I did that before I came home."

She nodded. "We need to pray extra hard for protection." She pushed herself up from the chair and gripped her walker. "If we're going to make it to church tomorrow, we'd better get some sleep."

It was a good idea, but sleep was probably going to be in short supply for both of them tonight.

When Jared returned to his bedroom, Justice stood looking up at him. His tail moved slowly back and forth, but there seemed to be sadness in his eyes.

Jared sank onto the bed and patted his leg. "Come here."

The German shepherd complied, and Jared held the dog's face in both hands. "I know, boy. You miss her. I do, too."

For two weeks after Miranda had been killed, Justice had stood vigil at the front door, leaving only to eat. Even after they'd returned to work, the dog had seemed depressed. Justice was his dog, his law enforcement partner, but Miranda had been the one who'd brought out his soft side with unending love and affection.

Now his dog was connecting with Kassie in the same way. Suddenly his odd behavior made sense.

The two women looked nothing alike. Miranda was blonde, Kassie dark-haired. Miranda was tall and large-boned, Kassie petite, a good eight inches shorter than his five foot eleven. But both had the same sweetness, the same love of dogs. Both were smart and competent, but with an underlying insecurity. Both had an inner strength that they didn't seem to recognize.

Jared heaved a sigh. "You like Kassie a lot. I like her, too. But she's not taking Miranda's place."

He released the dog's face to run a hand down his back. Justice tilted his head to the side and whined. The dog seemed to understand far more than Jared gave him credit for.

"Look, she's just a friend. I'm not ready for anything more."

He shook his head. He must be losing it. He was explaining his relationship with Kassie to his dog.

He lay down and pulled the sheet over himself. Justice settled down next to the bed. Another three hours of sleep would be nice, but it wasn't going to happen. He was too worried about Kassie.

The intruder likely wouldn't return tonight. But what about tomorrow night and the next night? He needed to convince her to get somewhere safe.

She'd insisted she had no idea who was after her or what they were looking for. She was telling the truth. He had no doubt.

It wasn't any consolation.

The thought of her having something bad men would kill to get was scary.

Her not having that something when the bad guys believed she did was downright terrifying.

Worshippers filed out of the white stucco building and into the sunlight. Jared walked next to Gram, Kassie on her other side.

For the past hour, he'd sat next to Kassie. Gram had seen to that, sliding into the row first so there would be no way she could be seated between them. It wasn't her first push to bring them together and wouldn't be her last. Fortunately, Kassie seemed good-natured about the overt matchmaking attempts.

He hadn't been disappointed in the seating arrangement. The spot next to him had been vacant for the past two years. Having it occupied, even by someone who was just a friend, had filled him with an unexpected sense of contentment.

As they walked toward the parking lot, Kassie leaned forward to look at him around Gram. "Kris and Gavin are coming for lunch. Would you guys like to join us?"

He glanced at his grandmother before accepting the invitation. It wasn't necessary. Gram's head bobbed up and down, and anticipation shone from her gray-blue eyes.

Jared smiled. Lunch with Kassie. As if Gram would refuse.

Personally, he couldn't think of a better way to spend a Sunday afternoon. He'd been alone for too many in recent months. He'd left his home in Pace because Gram had needed him. But maybe he was benefiting as much as Gram. Since coming to Pensacola, that gnawing loneliness seemed to be held at bay. Finding a new friend in Kassie didn't hurt, either.

He gave her a nod of approval. "Then it's set. Anything you want us to bring?"

"Just your appetite. And maybe Justice. Does he like other dogs?"

"Most of the time. He's met a few he didn't like."

"Kris will have Bella with her. Maybe we can introduce them in a neutral place, like the front yard. I think he'll like her."

He pressed the key fob to unlock his Suburban. They'd all ridden together. Another of Gram's ideas. She'd insisted it was silly to take two vehicles when they lived next door to one another. He hadn't had a valid counterargument.

When he pulled into Gram's driveway, the one next door was empty except for Kassie's Sorento. Kris apparently hadn't arrived. He'd wait until after Bella got settled in to bring Justice over.

Once inside Kassie's house, he unfolded Gram's walker and

helped her to one of the living room chairs. She lowered herself gently, hanging on to the chair's arms, then waved Jared away. "You go help Kassie. I'm fine."

He followed Kassie to the kitchen, where she took a stack of plates from the cupboard and opened the silverware drawer. "I have lunch under control. You can set the table."

He'd just finished when the front door creaked open, and a female voice announced they'd arrived.

Kassie pulled a casserole dish from the oven and glanced at him over one shoulder. "Can you go help her?"

He lifted a brow. *Help her?* As soon as he stepped into the living room, his question was answered. Kris was pushing the door shut with the sole of one shoe, a suitcase in each hand. Gavin stood behind her, clinging to one pant leg. The golden retriever was already crossing the room, headed for the sounds and smells in the kitchen.

After greeting Kris, then kneeling to encourage a high five from Gavin, he rose to introduce woman, child and dog to his grandmother.

He glanced at the suitcases. "You're moving in here?"

The lift of her brows held a touch of indignation. "Is that a problem?"

Yeah, it was. He was trying to convince Kassie to leave. Now her sister and nephew were moving in.

"No, except for the fact that I don't think any of you are safe here."

Kris frowned. "Why? Did something happen?"

Uh-oh. Maybe Kassie hadn't told her yet.

"I'll let Kassie fill you in." It wasn't his place.

Kris gave a sharp nod. "Whatever's going on, my presence here is temporary. I'm giving Shannon and her boyfriend a break." She pulled her lower lip between her teeth. "I get the distinct impression Carl doesn't like me being there."

Jared grabbed the handle of each suitcase, and Kris took

Gavin's hand and headed down the hall. He followed them into a bedroom and deposited the luggage next to the bed. As he headed back toward the living room, Kassie's voice drifted to him from the kitchen. She was talking to the dog like she would to an adored child. When he peered around the corner, Bella was lying on her back, one hind leg moving in excited circles as Kassie rubbed her belly. Definitely a dog person. No wonder Justice loved her so much.

Moments later, Kris stepped into the kitchen. "Whoa, what happened to the door?"

Kassie straightened. "Someone kicked it in last night. The alarm scared him off."

Kris's gaze shifted from her sister to Jared. "This is what you were talking about."

"Yeah. I wasn't trying to play dictator." He gave her a rueful smile.

"I understand."

Once they were all seated and the food had been blessed and passed, Kassie looked at Kris. "Shortly before the break-in, I got a call from Alyssa."

Kris frowned. "Wanting something, I suppose."

"Not this time. The night my phone was stolen, she got a call, someone demanding to know where Dad is."

"Did she tell them he's dead?"

"She tried. The caller believes he's alive. Made some veiled threats if we don't tell him where he is."

Kris rolled her eyes. Apparently, that was a common gesture when either of them talked about their younger sister. "Sounds like another one of her attention-getting ploys."

"Maybe. But supposedly she got this call shortly after she was talking to me and my phone was snatched. The timing seems too unlikely to be coincidence."

"So you think Dad's alive?"

"No. You don't fall overboard forty miles from shore and

make it back with the dinghy still attached to the boat. That's too far even for a strong swimmer like Dad. These guys apparently think he faked his death to try to disappear with something that belongs to them."

Kris released an unladylike snort. "That's assuming Alyssa didn't make the whole thing up. When have you ever believed anything she's said?"

When Kassie didn't respond, Kris continued. "If Dad was into something illegal, don't you think I'd have known?"

"Not if he wanted to keep it from you."

Kris glared at her. "I don't believe it. I knew him too well."

Gram laid down her fork and sat back in her chair. Jared recognized the pose. She'd been quietly listening to the conversation, but was ready to get involved.

"Sounds to me like Jared's right. Whatever's going on—until it's sorted out—neither of you girls are safe here. You both need to come and stay with Jared and me." She picked up her fork and resumed eating, as if that settled it.

Kassie lifted her brows. "Four adults, two large dogs and one child in a two-bedroom house?"

Gram shrugged. "It would be a little crowded, but we'd make it work."

Kassie shook her head. "I won't put you in danger, Ms. MaryAnn."

"None of us would be in danger, because Jared would protect us. And I've got his grandpa's .45 for when he's at work."

Jared stifled a chuckle. "And you know how to use it?" Gram had never liked guns, and while she was okay with it being in the house, she would never touch it.

Kris reached across the table to squeeze his grandmother's hand. "We really appreciate the offer, but I'm going back to my friend's house soon."

The conversation turned to lighter topics and stayed there

the rest of the meal. By the time they finished dessert, it was obvious Gram was getting fatigued.

He helped her up from the table. "How about if I walk you home for a nap?"

"Only if you agree to come back and enjoy your afternoon with Kassie."

He resisted his own eye roll. Could she be any more obvious? When he slid a sideways glance at Kassie, she was grinning. Kris was smiling, too.

"Agreed." He looked at Kris. "What do you think of me bringing Justice back and letting him and Bella get acquainted in the front yard?"

"Good idea."

Once he had Gram situated, he returned to Kassie's, Justice trotting beside him. The two dogs hit it off as well as Kassie had predicted, taking turns chasing each other around the yard. When they came back inside, Kris announced that it was time for Gavin's nap. Mother and son disappeared down the hall, Bella following.

Kassie leaned against the wall. "She'll be lying down with him. Since losing his father, he won't go to sleep alone."

"I understand. Death is hard for a little one to grasp." It wasn't any easier for adults.

Kassie pushed herself away from the wall. "I've got a two-person glider chair on the back patio, if you'd like to hang out outside."

"Perfect. That way we won't disturb the little one." The weather was perfect, too, typical for early May—sunny and warm, with a slight breeze.

Kassie poured them each a glass of iced tea and then frowned at the place where the back door used to be. "We'll have to go through the garage and around. Someone's coming to fix the door tomorrow morning."

"Good." With as many screws as he had in the plywood, it

was fairly secure. He'd also rigged up the sensor so if anyone tampered with the plywood it would trigger the alarm. But the sooner the repairs were made, the better.

He sat on the glider, and Kassie eased down next to him. Justice lay on the concrete at her feet.

He set the swing in motion, pumping it slowly with one foot. "How long do you expect your sister to be here?"

"Not long." She sighed. "All this has put a major wedge between us."

"I gathered that."

"Well, the wedge has always been there. It's just more obvious now. If I say anything that casts our father in a bad light, she accuses me of dishonoring his memory."

"She loved him and wants to think the best of him."

Kassie cast him a sideways glance, brows raised.

"I'm not taking sides. I just see where she's coming from." He paused. "Does your sister share your faith?"

"She did many years ago. Mom was the spiritual leader in our home. When she walked away from her faith, we three girls did, too. I came back two years ago, thanks to your grandma. Unfortunately, Kris never has. Any remnants of her faith that survived Mom's leaving took their final death blow when her husband was killed."

She looked down at her hands, resting in her lap. "Kris is right about my dad and me, though. We never got along. I was always closer to Mom. We had our music in common, and I felt like she at least loved me. Until she left, anyway. That kind of shattered the loving mother image."

He lifted an arm to let it rest against the back of the glider. "I can imagine."

"Now my dad's gone, too, and all I feel toward him is anger." She heaved a sigh. "You probably think I'm horrible."

He gave her shoulder a little shake. "Never."

She laughed, but it held sarcasm rather than humor. "Look

up *dysfunctional* in the dictionary, and you'll find a picture of my family. You probably came from a *Leave-It-to-Beaver* family."

He smiled. "They're not perfect, but I have awesome parents and grandparents." He paused. "I'm guessing yours is more normal than you realize."

"I don't know about that." She stared into the distance. "Over the past couple of years, I tried to make things right with my dad. Several times. But I was never successful, not on a permanent basis. He'd spent too many years finding fault with everything I did, and I'd built up a whole mountain of resentment. Now that he's gone, I feel like I didn't do enough. He died believing I hated him." She looked over at him, sorrow and regret swimming in her expressive blue eyes. "How do I deal with that?"

Jared's heart twisted. He was well-acquainted with the *what-ifs*. In the early morning hours when Miranda was killed, he'd been on his way home after his shift. He'd passed her jogging, waved at her, even blown her a kiss. What if he'd persuaded her to cut short her run and ride back to the house with him?

"Nobody's perfect. We've all made choices we wish we could undo." He pulled her to him in a sideways hug. "We change the things we can. The things we can't—well, we just have to release those to God."

She relaxed into him, snuggling against his side. A gentle breeze rustled the trees, a soothing backdrop to the soft creak of the swing as he continued its lazy back-and-forth motion. He was offering her comfort, and she was accepting it. But it was more than that. He was connecting with her on a level that was catching him off guard.

He wasn't ready to open his heart and let someone in again.

But for the first time since losing Miranda, the prospect didn't seem like a complete impossibility.

EIGHT

Kassie stepped from the dock onto the back of the Cabo. The sun shone from an almost cloudless sky, halfway through its descent.

As she approached the pilothouse, she breathed a sigh of relief. The door going into the cabin was locked, the same as it had been for the past two weeks. But that didn't stop the unease from blanketing her every time she walked up the dock.

She'd already gotten in an almost full day's work. An hour of prepping the boat for tomorrow's charter would wrap it up. Jared had insisted on helping her. She couldn't say she was disappointed.

She made her way down the companionway steps. She'd been so sure she wasn't ready for anything more serious than friendship. But sitting in the glider yesterday, snuggled against his side, had felt so right.

For Jared, what happened yesterday may have simply been one friend providing comfort to another. He hadn't tried to kiss her. Instead, they'd talked a little longer, and he'd gone home to his grandmother.

Kassie removed a sponge and soap from under the galley sink and began to wipe down surfaces. The boat tilted.

"Kassie? It's just me."

"I'm in the galley."

Jared moved down the four steps. "You look like you're hard at work."

"Yep, haven't stopped since I got up this morning. I got in a couple hours of accounting at the charter office, thanks to Buck agreeing to hang out. Then I dashed home to meet the handyman. The door is now fixed."

She moved to the sink to rinse the sponge. "After that, I headed to Kassie's Kuts for four hair appointments. My three hairdressers have been taking up my slack, but I've got a few customers who don't want anyone except me to touch their hair. Anyhow, this is the last chore of the day."

He smiled at her, warmth in his gaze. "You're pretty amazing, you know that?"

Yeah, he'd said that before. "Not everyone would agree with you."

"Tell me who would dispute your amazing-ness, and I'll be happy to set them straight."

"Besides my father? My ex."

"He's an idiot."

"How do you know? You've never met him."

"Two reasons. Number one, he didn't recognize your amazing-ness."

She grinned. "What's number two?"

"He let you get away."

His smile faded, and his brown eyes grew serious. He stepped closer and put both hands on her shoulders. "You're an amazing woman, Kassie. Don't ever let anyone try to convince you otherwise."

She looked up at him, searching for the truth of his words in his gaze. It held such admiration and sincerity she could almost believe what he'd just said. Warmth filled her chest, slowly spreading throughout her body. She was pretty pathetic, needing someone who barely knew her to provide confirmation of her worth. But right now, she'd take it.

"Thank you." She stepped away to retrieve her sponge. She'd been attracted to Jared immediately upon meeting him, but she needed to keep her head. Her life was complicated enough without throwing a new relationship into the mix. "Were you serious about wanting to help?"

"Absolutely. Give me a job."

"Clean the head?"

"I've never been afraid to get my hands dirty."

"Great. There's a sponge and cleanser under the sink."

Jared disappeared, and she returned to wiping the countertop. When she finished, she moved to the table and settee. Something sticky coated the end of one of the seat cushions, probably dried soft drink. She lifted out that one and the one next to it and placed them both on the table.

Great. The sticky mess was underneath, too. It had probably dribbled down into the under-seat storage areas. She removed the covers and swiped her sponge over the visible surfaces. "This is weird."

Jared looked out through the open doorway. "What's weird?"

"Check out these two compartments. This one is several inches shallower and looks like it has a false bottom." If not for the events of the past two weeks, she would assume the hidden area was space for wiring or plumbing or another innocuous purpose. "I've never noticed it before. We've got enough easily accessible storage, so this is the first time I've gotten into here. Help me take this out."

Jared knelt beside her, and together they pried the leather-covered panel up. She set it aside with shaking hands. Whatever she had hoped to find, the space was empty except for some dark-colored granules.

Jared picked up some of the substance and rolled it between his fingers. "Coffee grounds."

"How would they have gotten down here?"

"They were probably put there intentionally." His tone was low, heavy with meaning.

Kassie stared at him, brows drawn together. He seemed to know something she didn't. "Why?"

"Drug runners sometimes try to disguise the scent of drugs with coffee."

Kassie pushed herself to her feet, shaking her head. "No way. My dad had his faults, but I can't believe he was using his charter boat to run drugs."

Her own denial brought her up short. She sounded like her sister, refusing to believe what was right in front of her.

"But wouldn't drug-sniffing dogs have searched the boat before the Coast Guard turned it over to us?"

"The Coast Guard doesn't use drug-sniffing dogs as often as people think. Drug shipments on boats are large enough they don't need dogs to let authorities know they're there. Coast Guard dogs are more for sniffing out explosives. In this case, there was nothing suspicious. With the empty cans and bottles lying around and the dinghy still attached to the boat, the evidence painted a pretty clear picture."

She nodded, still struggling with the idea that her dad had been a drug runner. "Do you think he ripped some people off, and now they're determined to get their payment one way or another?"

If so, she was in a world of trouble. She had no idea where her father was—if he was still alive. And she didn't know where he'd put whatever he'd taken, or where to begin looking.

Before Jared could respond, his ringtone sounded from inside his shirt pocket. When he glanced at the screen, his sharp intake of breath indicated that he recognized the number but wasn't expecting the call.

"I have to take this."

As he climbed the companionway steps, she returned to her cleaning. Jared's voice drifted into the cabin.

"Hey, Wayne. You've got something on Miranda's case?"

Kassie paused in her scrubbing and looked through the open doorway. She had no clue who Miranda was, but something in Jared's tone had piqued her curiosity. His voice was tight, filled with both anticipation and apprehension. She shouldn't be eavesdropping, but if she wasn't supposed to hear the conversation, he should stand farther away than the pilothouse.

Over the next couple of minutes, he mostly listened, interjecting some "okays" and "I sees" every so often, then finally a "keep me posted."

When he stepped back into the galley, his face was three shades lighter than normal. He lifted a hand to run shaking fingers through his hair.

"Is everything okay?"

He leaned back against the counter and released a tension-filled breath. "They found the car that hit my wife."

Her stomach dropped. "Wait, you're married?"

"Was." He frowned. "Gram didn't tell you my wife was killed by a hit-and-run driver?"

"No." With everything Ms. MaryAnn had related, that was an important detail to leave out. It wasn't an oversight. She'd probably been afraid that if Kassie knew he'd be bringing that kind of baggage to a relationship, she would have run in the other direction. She'd been right.

Kassie shook her head. "I'm so sorry. When?"

"Two years ago. I was coming home from the night shift, passed her jogging when I drove into our neighborhood. I pulled into the driveway, stepped out of the car and heard a sickening thud. I knew instantly what had happened."

"That's awful." A minute passed in silence. Or maybe it was only a few seconds. A boulder had lodged in her stomach and wouldn't go away. She should say something, but nothing seemed appropriate. Jared had been happily married and had his wife torn from his side. Kassie couldn't say she knew how he felt, because she didn't.

Kris could. She'd been there and was still dealing with the fallout. She hadn't even considered dating since losing her husband. He was her soulmate and she didn't believe she'd ever find that kind of happiness again. Jared probably felt the same way. He wasn't commitment-phobic. He just hadn't been able to move beyond his loss.

She drew in a shaky breath. "The case has been unsolved all this time?"

"That's right. No witnesses. Shortly before pulling into my driveway, I saw an older Buick Roadmaster coming toward me but didn't think anything of it. A couple of my neighbors reported seeing the same car, but no one saw the accident."

"Now that they have the car, they'll be able to find the driver, right?"

"That's what we're hoping, but it's more complicated than that. The car was found about a mile into the woods near Muscogee, with the VIN number ground off and the plates removed. It's been sitting there a long time—lots of rust where tree limbs scraped the top and sides, rotted tires. But it matches the description given by witnesses."

"I hope they find the driver. You deserve justice."

"Miranda deserves justice." Several seconds passed in silence. Then he stood. "We've got a boat to clean, so we'd better get moving."

She gave him a tentative smile. "You're right."

Over the next forty-five minutes, they cleaned the boat, and conversation centered around what they were doing. She couldn't vouch for where Jared's thoughts were during the silent periods, but hers never strayed far from Miranda's accident, and the devastation it had to have caused in Jared's life.

After he followed her home and pulled into his grandmother's drive next door, she hollered another "Thank you" and unlocked her front door. When she stepped inside, Bella was the first to greet her, tail wagging. Soon, she flopped onto her back, and Kassie moved her hand over the silky golden fur of her belly.

Moments later, Gavin toddled in. "Aunt Kassie! You're home."

She wrapped her nephew in her arms and gave him a tight squeeze. Warmth filled her, the sense of comfort that should always be present when crossing the threshold of home.

She rose, still holding onto Gavin, and inhaled deeply. Kris was at it again in the kitchen. Soon they'd be leaving. But tonight, Kassie was thankful she hadn't had to walk into an empty house.

Yeah, she seriously needed to get a dog. Once Ms. Mary-Ann could get around better, she probably wouldn't mind letting the dog out while Kassie was at work. It would have to be something small or medium-sized. And calm. She wouldn't risk a seventy-pound bundle of energy knocking Ms. MaryAnn down and breaking the other hip. Maybe a corgi or beagle.

Kassie made her way toward the kitchen. She'd actually been entertaining thoughts of a relationship with Jared. His encouragement, the admiration and respect in his eyes. His saying she was amazing…and really meaning it. It was hard to resist. She'd put too much effort into trying to be good enough for the men in her life.

But eventually, Jared wouldn't be so impressed anymore and would start pointing out her faults. Trying to live up to the flesh-and-blood Miranda Miles would be hard enough. She wasn't about to settle for playing second best to a memory.

No, she could never be what he needed. She would support him as a friend. She'd listen to him and encourage him in any way she could.

But she'd never be able to compete with his dead wife.

She wouldn't even try.

* * *

Kassie squeezed her eyes shut, trying to block out the heavy pounding reverberating around her.

Not just pounding. Barking, too. Someone needed to kill the jackhammer and muzzle the dog. She groaned and rolled onto her back.

Bella!

Her eyes snapped open. Kris and Gavin were sleeping in the next room, Bella with them. Something was wrong.

She bolted upright, swallowing hard against a wave of dizziness and nausea. Her head hurt, too.

The pounding came again.

"Kris?"

She rose from the bed with a moan, one hand clutched to her stomach, the other holding the side of her head. What was wrong with her?

As she stepped from her room, the spare bedroom door swung open and Bella bolted down the hall. Kris stood in the opening looking as rough as Kassie felt. "What's going on?"

"I don't know." She stumbled down the hall, hanging onto the wall for support. "Someone's out front."

Frenzied barking came from the living room. Bella paced in front of the door, sharp barks showing her agitation. Kassie separated the blinds at the window to peer outside. A fire truck and ambulance were parked along the road, a police car in the driveway, its red-and-blue lights flashing in the darkness. What had happened?

She jumped at renewed pounding, so close.

"Police. Open the door."

She glanced over her shoulder, but Kris had disappeared, likely to check on Gavin.

When Kassie swung open the door, the dog stopped barking, but a piercing squeal filled the silence. She'd forgotten to turn off the alarm. She punched the four numbers into the keypad next to the door and turned back to the two officers standing on her porch. Behind them were a pair of firemen and two emergency medical personnel.

She looked from one to another, confusion further clouding her already foggy brain.

"What's going on?"

One of the officers responded—Thornhill, according to his name tag. "Your car is running in your garage. This place might be full of carbon monoxide."

"My car? But…how?"

Kris stepped up beside her, now holding Gavin. "It wasn't running when we went to bed."

"You should all come outside, get some fresh air, just in case."

Kassie nodded. Carbon monoxide. That would explain the fogginess and headache. But it didn't explain how her car was running when her keys were in her bedroom.

The officers backed up to allow them to exit. Kris stepped out with Gavin and called Bella.

Kassie hesitated. "If we're going to the garage, I need my keys."

Officer Thornhill gave a sharp nod. "Just don't dally."

"Believe me, I won't." She'd hold her breath all the way to her room and back if she could.

A minute later, she stepped outside, keys gripped in one hand. As she approached the large metal door, the rumble of the Kia's engine reached her from inside the garage. She rounded the corner, ready to slide the key into the lock on the side door, and froze. Someone had busted a fist-sized hole in the bottom corner of the glass inches from the door knob.

Officer Thornhill stopped her. "Don't touch anything."

His partner walked away and returned a couple of minutes later with a fingerprint kit and two pairs of latex gloves. After handing one to Thornhill, he donned his own.

Thornhill opened the door, and his gaze circled the frame. "This door wasn't protected by the alarm."

"No, just the door leading from the garage into the house."

She'd thought that if every window and door to the house had sensors, she'd be safe. Bad assumption.

While the others waited outside, Kassie and Officer Thornhill stepped into the garage. She flipped the light switch, and the officer shone his flashlight through the Sorento's passenger window, chasing away the shadows inside the vehicle. There was damage around the base of the steering column.

He tilted his head toward the rear of the vehicle. "Open the garage door so we can get some fresh air in here. If you get me a screwdriver, I'll shut your car off."

Kassie hurried to the door entering the house and pressed the button. The large metal door rose along its tracks. When she'd produced a flathead screwdriver from the nearby tool bin, Officer Thornhill opened the passenger door and leaned across the seat. Several seconds later, the engine died.

Kassie watched him close the door. "Someone hot-wired my car." They could easily have stolen it.

But that wasn't their intent. The plan was to fill the garage with carbon monoxide and possibly asphyxiate the people inside, including Kris and Gavin.

"Officer Thornhill?" The voice floated through the now open garage door. "You need to look at this."

Two firemen stood there. Kris was walking with the paramedics toward the ambulance, likely to be checked out. Gavin's little arms wrapped the back of her neck, and his stockinged feet bounced on either side of her hips. Bella trotted beside them.

Kassie followed Officer Thornhill along the Kia's passenger's side to the large opening and glanced back at her car. Foil tubing was taped to the end of the muffler, snaking from there to the house's AC ductwork where it emerged from the air handler. Her stomach dropped.

Whoever was responsible hadn't just started the car and hoped the carbon monoxide wafted into the house. They'd piped the muffler into the air handler to make sure it did. It wasn't warm enough to run the AC, but she had the system's fan on to circulate air. Anyone entering the garage or standing outside would know the system was running.

But that didn't explain how they got her car started without her key.

"I thought newer cars couldn't be hot-wired." Although hers wasn't new. It had passed the one-decade mark two years ago.

Thornhill nodded. "You're right. Anything made after the midnineties can't be hot-wired, because the car's computer shuts everything down."

"So how did this happen?"

"There are a couple of ways thieves can get around it. One way is to swap out the ECU, reader and chip with ones from a junkyard, then break the ignition lock, rip off the switch and hold the replacement chip by the reader. After that, they can turn the ignition switch with a screwdriver, and *voilà*, the car starts."

Kassie shook her head. This was all beyond her ability to comprehend. Someone had tried to kill her tonight. Kris and Gavin and Bella could have been collateral damage. If the authorities hadn't shown up when they had, the outcome could have been totally different.

She looked up at Thornhill. "Who discovered my car running? How did you guys know to respond?"

"Dispatch received an anonymous call. The caller gave this address and hung up."

Another police cruiser turned into the driveway and screeched to a halt behind Thornhill's. The driver door swung open and Jared hurried toward her with little more than a cursory glance at his fellow officers. What she saw in his eyes didn't look like mere professional concern. Her stomach did a somersault. For someone who was convinced she didn't want a romantic relationship, her heart wasn't cooperating.

He put his hands on her shoulders. "Are you guys all right? I was tied up on another call when this one was dispatched."

Kassie filled him in on what had happened, ending with what she'd learned about the 911 call.

Jared frowned. "Why would someone go to all this trouble and then call it in?"

Kassie lifted her shoulders in a slow shrug. "Maybe they changed their mind." But that didn't ring true. These people would have no compunction about killing her. But if they believed she had information, they needed her alive.

"We don't have those answers," Thornhill said. "We just got here and haven't searched the garage and surrounding area yet."

Over the next several minutes, Thornhill checked each surface in the beam of his flashlight while his partner dusted for prints. The sixty-watt bulb in the center of the ceiling left too many areas in shadow.

While the men did their work, Kassie waited in the driveway, Jared next to her. Whether he was staying back because it wasn't his case or he was simply remaining beside her for moral support, she didn't know. She liked to think it was the latter.

Finally, Thornhill reached along the side of the air handler and pulled out a three-by-three Post-it note with one latex-covered hand.

Jared stiffened next to her. "What does it say?"

Thornhill lifted his gaze from the note to Jared's face. His mouth was set in a frown, his eyes narrowed in concern.

While Kassie waited for his response, her heart pounded

in her ears, intensifying the headache she already had. Whatever was written there, it wasn't good.

When Thornhill finally spoke, a cold lump formed in her core.

"Next time there won't be a 911 call."

NINE

Jared chased Gavin around the front yard of the Ashbaugh home, fingers curved like claws and growling sounds emanating from between his bared teeth. The little boy's happy squeals left no doubt about how much he was enjoying the activity.

Four days had passed since Kassie, Kris and Gavin had gone to the emergency room with carbon monoxide poisoning. Even though the exposure had shown up on their blood work, after a few hours on oxygen, they'd been sent home, with instructions to call if symptoms persisted. Even Bella had gotten a clean bill of health from the vet.

Kris and Gavin had gone back to Shannon's house, in spite of the tension with the boyfriend. When Jared had expressed concern over Gavin's safety, Kris had assured him there was no threat to her or her son.

With another squeal, the boy ran around the back side of a large oak, his hysterical giggles giving away his location. He definitely hadn't learned the concept of stealth.

Jared scooped him up amid laughter and squeals of delight and hugged him to his chest. He and Miranda had never had children. Being an only child, he didn't even have nephews and nieces to spoil. That left his friends' children.

He lowered Gavin to the ground and took his hand. "Let's go find Mommy and Aunt Kassie."

Since the incident at her house, Kassie had been staying with Gram and him. Even there, she hadn't been able to relax. He hadn't, either. The note left in her garage had promised a "next time." It wasn't a question of *if* but *when*.

For the past several days, he'd been doing his own search, going through records on local criminals involved in assaults and robberies, looking for potential suspects. So far, no one had stood out.

The offer he'd made of his room had never come to fruition. He'd tried, but since Kassie slept when almost everyone else in the Central time zone did, she'd insisted on taking the couch and leaving him the bedroom where he could draw the drapes and have semidarkness and quiet. He'd lost the argument.

That wasn't the only place he was losing. He'd almost decided to consider a romantic relationship with her. She'd been thinking about it, too. When they'd sat together on the glider and she'd nestled into his side, when they'd been on her boat and he'd told her how amazing she was—both times, her actions and demeanor had said she wanted more than friendship.

Now, something was different. The change had come with the call from Wayne. He could guess what was bothering her. It wasn't that she expected him, at thirty-three, to have never been involved with someone. It was the fact that Miranda's and his relationship had not ended by choice.

He and Gavin climbed the porch steps together. They'd stopped by the house because Kris needed to pick up some items for her and Gavin before heading back to Shannon's. She'd made the smart choice and asked Kassie to meet her there. Kassie had made the even smarter choice and asked him. Though he wasn't in uniform, his service revolver was secured in the holster hidden by his T-shirt, and all the while playing with Gavin, he'd kept watch on their surroundings. He wouldn't let down his guard, even though there hadn't been any threats since the carbon monoxide incident. Unfortunately, there hadn't been any breaks, either. None of the prints lifted from Kassie's purse or her garage had produced any matches.

When they stepped into the foyer, soft female voices drifted to them from the direction of the kitchen. As he and Gavin approached, the voices grew louder, the words clearer.

"Stop beating yourself up. It's not your fault." Kassie's voice held a lot of sympathy.

He hesitated. This was a conversation he shouldn't interrupt, especially considering the friction that often existed between the twins.

"I can't." Kris heaved a sigh, audible even from where he stood. "I've never told you this, but recently Dad's drinking had gotten worse. Since I wouldn't let him drink around Gavin and me, he'd often stay away two or three days at a time, sleeping it off on the boat. Now he's gone, and I can't help feeling responsible. If he'd been at home, he wouldn't have drowned."

"Kris." Kassie's tone held firmness. "You know what it was like growing up under the shadow of alcoholism. Dad made his choices. Your first responsibility is to protect your son, and that's exactly what you did."

Jared squeezed Gavin's hand and bent over. "Psst. I'll race you upstairs."

Gavin giggled and took off, little feet padding against the hardwood floor. He climbed the stairs the same way all little ones did—stopping with both feet on the same stair tread before proceeding to the next. Jared stayed far enough behind to not overtake him, but close enough to catch him should he stumble in his haste to get away.

When the little boy made it to the top, he ran full speed down the hall, not stopping until he reached the closed door at the end. He stretched to wrap both hands around the doorknob. A few seconds later, the door swung inward.

Jared peered inside. A mahogany four-poster bed occupied the room, along with a matching dresser and chest of drawers.

A heavy desk sat in the corner. The walls held artwork with themes of fishing, hunting and the outdoors in general. This was Bobby Ashbaugh's room.

A shirt and pair of pants were draped over an upholstered chair in the corner, and the bed, though made, looked as if the sheet and bedspread had been tossed over the pillows, no tucking attempted. Maybe Kris was keeping the room unchanged, a quasi shrine to the father she'd adored.

Jared peered in at the little boy, who was now running in tight circles around an eight-by-ten rug next to the bed. "Are you allowed in here, buddy?"

"Uh-huh."

Jared stepped inside. If they were somewhere they shouldn't be, he'd deal with the fallout later. He wouldn't let Gavin take the heat, no matter what the little boy had told him.

Gavin crumpled to the rug, lying on his back. "Tickle monster!"

Jared approached, fingers curling and straightening in a slow rhythm. Gavin squealed even louder, arms extended, feet kicking.

Jared dropped to his knees and continued the motions with his hands, moving them closer to the little boy's ribs. "Tickle monster!"

Gavin pulled the corner of the rug on top of him and tried to roll over. Jared gave him a nudge and soon had him rolled into a tight cocoon, the entire rug occupied except one corner still covering the hardwood floor.

Happy sounds, now muffled, continued to leak out the end of the rug while Jared stared at a narrow gap in the floorboards. It ran about two feet, then jutted off at a ninety-degree angle before turning another corner. At the far end was a small canvas loop.

He sat back on his heels, staring at what was obviously a secret compartment in the floor. Did Kris and Kassie know it was there? Or did Kris know but Kassie didn't? If so, would she try to keep him from seeing what was hidden beneath?

It was a chance he'd have to take. He didn't have a warrant, so if he lifted out that section of flooring without Kris's consent and Bobby Ashbaugh reappeared and faced charges, anything Jared found wouldn't be admissible in court.

He unrolled the rug, exposing the still giggling child, but when Gavin's eyes met his, the giggles trickled away. The little boy seemed to notice that the playful atmosphere had dissipated and something heavy hung in the air.

Jared took both of his hands and lifted him to his feet. "Let's go see Mommy and Aunt Kassie. They're probably done talking now."

When they got to the bottom of the stairs, the tone of the voices was much lighter. Jared even heard his own name mentioned but couldn't make out the rest of the words.

He cleared his throat loudly enough for them to hear, then released Gavin's hand. "Go find Mommy."

The little boy shot away from him, squeals and giggles renewed. When Jared reached the kitchen, both women were seated at the table. Kris had angled her chair to make room for her son to climb onto her lap, and Bella was lying at her feet.

Kassie motioned toward two duffel bags. "We're ready when you are."

"There's something you both need to see first."

Kassie's smile faded. Kris slid Gavin from her lap, lips pressed into a straight line.

Jared climbed the stairs with Bella and the three of them in tow and led them to the room at the end of the hall. Keeping his eyes on Kris, he folded back the rug, exposing what he'd found. Something flitted across her features, so brief he couldn't say whether it was surprise or concern. Maybe both.

"Did either of you know about this?"

Kassie shook her head, her slack jaw confirming her denial.

Kris crossed her arms, a sudden hardness in her features. "So you decided to search my house on the pretext of playing with my son. Is that even legal?"

He bristled at the accusation. "I *was* playing with your son. He came in here on his own, pulled the corner of the rug over himself and tried to roll up inside. When he couldn't do it, I helped him." He paused. "Did you know about this?" He stared at her, silently daring her to deny it. "You could have all died the other night. If you know anything, you need to come clean and stop covering for your father."

Kris narrowed her eyes, but that didn't hide the anger simmering there. "I'm *not* covering for him."

"You grew up in this house and have lived here for the past year as an adult. Did you know this was here?"

Gavin pressed himself against his mother's side and slid his thumb into his mouth. He could probably feel the friction between the adults in the room.

Kris answered without wavering. "No. There's always been a rug there. Dad insisted on cleaning his own room, so I never had reason to move the rug. This is the first time I've seen the floor underneath."

Kassie dropped to her knees and reached for the canvas loop. "Does someone want to help me lift this out rather than just staring at it?"

Kris disentangled the little fingers from the hem of her blouse and knelt next to her sister. When they had the rectangular panel raised at an angle, Jared helped them set it aside. Three metal boxes occupied the space.

Kris lifted one out and tried to slide the small silver lever to the side. "It's locked."

She lifted the second one out, and Kassie removed the third. All were locked.

Kris stood and moved toward her father's desk. "He has to

have keys somewhere, either here or at the office. Since the boxes are here, the keys probably are, too."

While Kassie looked through the large walk-in closet, Kris searched each of the desk drawers. When that produced nothing, she crawled under the desk. "Bingo. There's a pouch taped here."

Jared moved closer. She had shifted to a seated position, her back against one side of the desk. One arm was raised as she fiddled with something on the underside of the center drawer. Then she held out a hand. Three small silver keys dangled from a string looped around her index finger.

Kassie took them from her and tried a key in one of the locks. It didn't turn. The second key did. When she raised the lid, the air whooshed from her lungs. She'd apparently been holding her breath.

Jared stepped to one side of her and Kris to the other to peer into the box. Bound stacks of bills filled the space. Based on the top one in each stack, they were all fifties and hundreds. Each of the other two boxes held the same.

Kris shook her head. "There are thousands of dollars here."

Kassie still stared into one of the boxes. "Tens or hundreds of thousands."

"Why didn't he put it in the bank? He wasn't one of those old people who thought his money was safer buried in coffee cans or stuffed inside the mattress."

Kassie frowned at her sister. "He didn't put it in the bank because he couldn't justify where it came from."

"What if it came from the charter business?"

"We've both been involved with Ashbaugh Charters enough to know we don't do this amount of business. We never have."

"Maybe the money wasn't Dad's. He might not have even known it was here."

Kassie sighed. "Kris, come on."

Kris spun on her. "Don't *come on* me. This house was in

Mom's family long before Mom and Dad even met. Maybe Grandma and Grandpa were the ones who didn't trust banks."

Kassie looked into the box she held. "This wasn't put here by Grandma and Grandpa."

"How do you know?"

"Some of these top bills are dated 2010 and later. Grandma and Grandpa left and we moved in way before that."

Jared watched the exchange without comment. The evidence was piling up, the weight of it smothering the last of Kris's objections. She'd been making excuses since everything started, trying to hold onto the image of the man she loved— a father with his faults, but still a good man.

That image was a façade. Her father wasn't just an alcoholic. He was a drug runner whose illegal activities had put his entire family at risk.

As Kris blinked back tears she was trying not to shed, Kassie scooted closer to her and put an arm around her shoulders. Seeing the hurt in both of their eyes twisted Jared's heart.

But he had a job to do. What they held was likely drug money. If it was marked, it could be used to solve not only this case, but possibly others.

He cleared his throat. "This needs to be reported."

Kris nodded. "I figured as much."

"If it's not marked and there's nothing connecting it to a crime, it'll likely be returned. Don't count on it anytime soon, though."

Kassie stood and moved toward the hall. "I'll make the call. We don't want this kind of money sitting in the house."

Downstairs, they all took a seat in the living room. Soon the police would arrive and take the three boxes into evidence. Was that money what the men were after?

Not likely. If Bobby Ashbaugh really did fake his death and abscond with something, the odds of him slipping back into the house unseen to hide it were slim. So what did he have?

With that kind of money stashed away, what would prompt him to rip someone off?

Whether he was dead or alive, the men weren't likely to give up until they had what they wanted. They'd left clear warning in Kassie's garage—it was only a matter of time until they struck again.

Hopefully the find under the floorboards would lead somewhere.

Because they really needed a break in the case.

Kassie sat back in her chair and watched pages drop into the printer tray. It had been a busy day, with too many left-brain activities for a Monday. She'd started out the morning at Kassie's Kuts, catching up the bookkeeping and making a bank deposit.

Now she was at the charter office doing much more intensive accounting. She'd decided to go back eighteen months. A year and a half should provide plenty of information for a potential buyer.

She pulled the sheets from the printer tray and slid them into the three-hole punch. "Balance sheet, income statement, bank reconciliation. Two months down, sixteen to go."

She put them into the binder in front of the prior month and looked at the clock. *5:52 p.m.?* How did it get so late?

"Time flies when you're having fun." Except she wasn't. Not even a little. A career in accounting had never been on her radar.

But now that she was in the mode, maybe she could keep going a little while longer. She just had to be out of there before dark or Jared would have her hide.

She frowned. She'd always been a do-whatever-it-takes-to-get-it-done kind of person, even if doing whatever it took involved late nights. Having someone trying to kill her was putting a crimp in her schedule.

She pulled out the folder for the next month. Like the others, it was pitifully thin—just the bank statements she'd printed, some gas and other receipts, merchant statements for credit cards processed and sketchy records of charters done.

"One month at a time." She'd already gotten through two. She'd get the others done, too.

She finished entering all of the bank deposits for the month and looked at the clock again. Six thirty. She'd have to call it a night.

She pulled her phone from her purse. Instead of running Kris or Buck back out just to make sure she got to her car safely, she had talked to Don at one of the nearby businesses. She'd told him they'd had a break-in and a friend was concerned about her leaving alone. He'd said he'd be happy to play bodyguard for a few minutes.

Before she could place the text, her phone rang in her hand. She smiled at Jared's name on the screen. Unfortunately, her determination to limit their relationship to friendship didn't keep her from getting all fluttery every time she talked to him. If she didn't get a grip soon, it was going to be easier to give in and let the chips fall where they may.

She greeted him as she rose from the desk.

"Where are you?"

"Getting ready to leave the office."

"I thought you'd be home by now." There was no annoyance in his tone, just concern.

"I was on a roll, playing 'Fun with Numbers.' Didn't want to stop. But I'm leaving as soon as we hang up."

"You're alone?"

She stepped into the hall, swiping the light switch on the way out of her dad's office. "Someone I know who's working nearby is going to see me to my car."

"Good. Your dinner is in the fridge."

"Awesome." She hadn't had to cook dinner for herself since moving in to Ms. MaryAnn's.

"I've got to get ready for my shift. But if you're leaving right away, I should still be here."

As soon as she ended the call, she sent the text to Don. The return one came a half minute later. At your service.

Before unlocking the front door, she peered through the glass. To her left, the sun sat low on the horizon, its bottom edge resting atop one of the buildings. Daylight would be fading soon. Don hurried across the street toward her. She set the alarm and stepped outside. By the time she'd finished locking the door, he was standing next to her.

She smiled up at him. "Thanks for doing this."

"Don't mind a bit."

He fell into step beside her. Totally unarmed, slightly built and almost as old as her father, he wouldn't be much of a deterrent if someone really wanted to attack her, but there was safety in numbers.

Once she was in her driver's seat with the engine running, he stepped back and lifted a hand in farewell. "Stay safe."

"I will." In recent weeks, safety had become her number one priority.

Five minutes later, she stopped in Ms. MaryAnn's driveway next to Jared's cruiser. If he didn't leave soon, he'd be late for his shift. That was another reason she'd had to set aside the accounting when she had. He wouldn't want to leave until she was safely inside.

Before unlocking the car door, she peered through the window to check her surroundings. Nothing looked amiss. After readying the house key, she took another glance around the yard and stepped out.

She'd covered less than half the distance to the front porch when a rustle sounded behind her. She swiveled her head, a scream welling up inside. Before she could release it, a strong arm wrapped her torso, and the sharp edge of a knife pressed against her throat.

"Don't move." Warm breath brushed her ear, carrying the scent of cigarette smoke and chewing gum. "Make a sound, and I'll slit you from ear to ear and leave you to bleed out in your neighbor's driveway. You understand?"

She gave a couple of jerky bobs of her head, eyeing the front of the house. Her heart slammed against her ribcage, and her breaths came in rapid pants. Where was Jared? Would he even hear her if she screamed?

No, she couldn't scream. The man had already warned her.

"Unlock your car. We're going for a ride, and you're gonna tell me where your father's hiding."

She swallowed hard. She couldn't tell him what she didn't know. *God, help me.*

Without releasing her or lowering the knife, he forced her toward the car. She fingered the key fob, resting her thumb on the green "unlock" button. What if she armed the alarm instead, then used her key to unlock the car? The alarm would sound the instant she opened the door.

No, he'd probably cut her. She couldn't risk it. She pressed the green button and the locks clicked.

"Open the door."

She did as he instructed. A sliver of hope cut through her despair. Maybe she could lock herself inside before he could get in and then blow the horn until Jared came out.

Still holding the knife at her throat, he reached behind him with his left hand to open the back door. Hope withered as quickly as it had sprouted.

He gave her a shove, lowering the knife at the same time, and she tumbled into the car. As soon as her feet were clear, he slammed the door and started to climb into the seat behind her.

In a sudden spark of desperation, she threw her purse to the passenger floorboard and scrambled across the console. Once outside, she released a long, terrified scream. Jared would hear her, even if Ms. MaryAnn had the TV on.

She couldn't run inside the house. The man would grab her before she even slid her key into the lock. Instead, she needed to evade him until Jared got outside. She sprinted toward the park across the street. She had to remain within sight of Jared when he bolted out the front door. Seconds wasted looking for her could be the difference between life and death.

She ran across De Soto Street, still screaming. Every time she fell silent to take another gasping breath, curses filled the air behind her.

"You're gonna pay for this." The angry words sent panic ricocheting through her. He might kill her in a fit of rage and look elsewhere for the information he wanted.

As she ran through the park, footsteps pounded the concrete path behind her. He was gaining on her. She couldn't look, wouldn't do anything to sacrifice even a sliver of her momentum.

When she got to the round raised bed at the center of the park, she circled it to double back. Across the street, Ms. Mary-Ann's front door swung open.

"Jared!" She screamed his name, loud and long, even though he hadn't stepped outside yet.

The next moment, open palms slammed into her back, sending her careening toward the concrete. A half second later, a heavy body fell on top of her, pressing the breath from her lungs.

Her attacker flipped her over, his face contorted in rage. This was it, he was going to kill her. He raised his fist. But it didn't hold the knife. Maybe he wasn't…

The fist came down with lightning speed and slammed into the side of her head. Pain exploded through her skull.

Blackness hovered at the edges of her vision—rolling, expanding, deepening, until it consumed everything.

TEN

Jared swung open the front door, pulse pounding in his ears. He'd been in his bedroom, having just finished donning his uniform and clipping on his duty belt, when he heard screams. So he'd snatched up his weapon and run down the hall, hollering for Justice.

Kassie's Sorento was in the drive. Both the rear driver-side door and front passenger door were wide open. But Kassie was gone. He radioed in a possible kidnapping. If he was wrong, he'd straighten it out later.

Justice released a whine, body rigid with tension.

"Where is she, boy?"

Justice barked, nose pointed toward the park across the street. Jared's heart almost stopped. In front of the large raised bed with its knee-high brick wall, a stocky figure was rising, a much slighter person in his arms. Behind him, a light post rose from the center of the bed, its bulb now burning. In the final remnants of daylight, he couldn't identify either figure.

But he had no doubt. The woman was Kassie. An unconscious Kassie, judging from the way her arms and legs dangled as the man carried her away.

"Justice, pursue."

Justice sprang forward, legs a blur. Jared took off after him, weapon drawn, ready to use if needed.

"Stop! Police!"

The man spun, tossing Kassie away from him. She landed on her side in a crumpled heap.

As much as Justice loved her, he shot past her without hesitation. He was a dog on a mission.

Without his burden, her assailant ran even faster. But he was no match for the dog's speed. Justice overtook him in seconds and in one flying leap, clamped his jaws around the man's forearm.

Rage and pain erupted from him in one agonized scream. He tried to twist away, but Justice held him firmly.

"Get him off of me!" He fell to his knees and raised his hands. "Call him off."

Justice could hold the man a few seconds longer. He had to check on Kassie. *God, please let her be okay.*

He knelt next to her and checked her pulse. It pounded against his fingertips in a firm rhythm. He blew out a breath, his tension uncoiling. When he drew his hand back, there was moisture on his fingertips. Blood.

A faint reddish line about two inches in length marked the side of her throat, a deep scratch. Or a cut. Had her assailant held a knife to her throat? Heat built in his chest. The man was twice her weight and probably three times her strength. What had he done to her? *God, please let her be okay.* It was the second time he'd murmured that prayer in less than a half minute. He wouldn't stop until she woke up and assured him she was all right.

He radioed dispatch again to request an ambulance and made his way to the suspect. He was kneeling in the grass, sitting back on his heels, face contorted. When apprehending someone, Justice wasn't gentle.

Jared didn't feel an ounce of pity. He removed the handcuffs from his belt and pulled the suspect's free arm behind him, clicking one cuff closed around that wrist. He didn't resist.

"Justice, release."

The dog turned loose of the other arm and sat.

"Good boy."

As Jared finished cuffing the suspect, he read him his rights. Justice looked back at the motionless lump next to the sidewalk and whined.

"Go ahead, boy. Go check on Kassie."

The squeal of sirens began faintly and then grew in volume. Soon strobing red and blue danced over the road a short distance away. A half minute later, two police cars skidded to a stop at the edge of Reus Street bordering the park.

The officers jumped out and approached, and Jared passed off the suspect to them. "I'm going to check on the victim. I believe the suspect tried to kidnap her. Also, he has a bite on his right forearm that'll need attending to."

As soon as he reached Kassie, he knelt behind her. Justice had lain down in front of her, legs tucked under him. The side of his face rested next to Kassie's, and his body stretched along her torso and thighs. She still hadn't moved.

Jared put a hand on her shoulder. "Kassie? Can you hear me?"

She released a small moan. Another siren sounded in the distance.

He gently squeezed her shoulder. "Justice and I are here. Help is on the way."

The piercing squeal grew louder. Jared heaved a sigh of relief when the red-and-white truck came into view, *Escambia County EMS* painted on its side.

Kassie moaned again, this time more loudly. Maybe she was coming around. She lifted an arm to press her hand to the side of her head. When she let it fall again, her hand came to rest on the dog's back. She opened one eye.

"Justice?" The word was slurred. One side of her mouth lifted in a hint of a smile. "Sweet boy."

Thank you, Jesus! He tamped down the urge to pick her up and hug her. "The ambulance is here. You're going to be okay."

Two emergency medical personnel approached with a stretcher. Jared straightened and stepped back. "Justice, come."

Justice made eye contact with him before rising to plod over to him. The dog never failed to obey a command. But that obedience was reluctant this time.

One of the paramedics knelt next to Kassie and put a hand on her shoulder. "Ma'am?"

"Mmm-hmm." Her eyes remained closed.

"Can you tell us what happened?"

"Uh-uh."

"Just lie here a few minutes. We're going to check your vitals." He slid a blood pressure cuff around her arm and an oxygen sensor on the end of one finger.

Over the next minute, she seemed to rouse a little more. The paramedic removed both the cuff and the sensor. "Pressure and oxygen are normal. Do you hurt anywhere?"

"My head."

"Anywhere else?"

"Uh-uh."

"Did something happen?"

Her brows drew together, as if she was struggling to remember. "I don't know."

"Any trouble breathing?"

She sucked in a slow breath and released it. "No."

"Can you try rolling onto your back?"

She did as instructed, and her eyes flickered open.

"Do you hurt anywhere now?"

"My head, maybe my neck." Her legs and arms twitched, as if she was trying to take inventory. "That's all."

He shone a penlight into her eyes for a few seconds before redirecting it to the side, then did it two more times. Jared waited, the knot in his chest releasing slightly. Her answers were encouraging. Maybe she didn't have anything more serious than a concussion.

When the emergency medical personnel had finished their assessment, one of them again laid a hand on her shoulder. "We're going to take you to the emergency room. You probably have a concussion, but you need to get thoroughly checked out."

After they had loaded her onto the gurney, Jared stepped up beside her.

She reached for his hand. "What happened to me?"

"I'm not sure. I heard you screaming. When Justice and I ran outside, you were already in the park, unconscious. Your charter customer was carrying you away."

Suddenly her eyes widened. "I was walking to the house when he grabbed me, put a knife to my throat. He said we were going to go for a ride and I was going to tell him where my father was hiding."

He nodded. She hadn't explained how she'd gotten from the driveway with a knife at her throat, to lying in the park unconscious. That would be a story for later.

The medical personnel wheeled the gurney toward the ambulance, but Kassie didn't release his hand. "Are you coming to the hospital?"

"I will later. Soon." He would go to the station to report for duty, write his report and maybe see if he could talk to the suspect. He wasn't a responding officer tonight, but he had been on previous calls. Besides, he'd been trying to discover this guy's identity ever since he saw him leaving the marina. Once finished, he'd go see Kassie.

"Can you get my purse? It's on the floorboard of my car. I need to call Kris."

He jogged back to his grandmother's house and looked inside the Kia's open passenger door. Kassie's purse was lying on its side, some of its contents strewn across the floor. He stuffed her phone, checkbook and several pens into the open zippered compartment and hurried back to the ambulance. When he arrived, they'd already loaded her inside. One of the men took her purse from him and handed it in to her.

She gave him an appreciative smile. "Thanks."

A sudden lump lodged in his throat. She looked so fragile lying there, dark ponytail flowing over the side of the sheet under her, her usually tanned skin pasty. His chest tightened at the thought of leaving her. For the first hour or so, they would run tests—X-rays, CT scan and who knew what else. That would give him time to report for duty and write his report on what happened this evening.

No, he wasn't even going to do that much. He'd call in right now and forego his shift altogether. Then he'd follow the ambulance to the hospital.

Kassie still wasn't safe. The man who'd attacked her on the boat had been apprehended, but there was someone still out there who was as much of a threat as the guy being hauled away.

Jared followed one paramedic to the cab of the ambulance and waited while he slid into the driver seat. "The man that attacked this lady tonight, he's got a partner. So it would be a good idea to give hospital security a heads-up."

"Will do."

Maybe the other man knew nothing about the events that had transpired tonight. Or maybe he was nearby watching and knew that Kassie was on her way to the hospital.

Let him come. He'd be walking into a trap. Because there was no way anyone was going to get to Kassie.

Not on his watch.

Jared rapped on the doorjamb, a bouquet of carnations and baby's breath in the other hand. When he stepped into Kassie's room, she was in a semi-seated position, the back of her bed raised forty-five degrees.

While the doctor had conducted his follow-up with her, Jared had made a quick trip to the hospital gift shop.

"You're back." Kassie's gaze shifted from his face to the flowers, and her mouth turned up in a pleased smile.

The doctor left the room, and Jared placed what he'd bought on the rolling table beside her bed and took her hand. "What did the doctor say?"

"He's sending me home today."

"Good. How's your headache?"

"A little better. I suspect I have the painkillers to thank for that."

"Whatever the case, I'm glad you're feeling better."

Last night's X-ray and CT scan hadn't revealed anything of serious concern, but they'd diagnosed her with a concussion and suggested she remain overnight for observation. She was obviously ready for the stay to be over. Knowing Kassie, she was thinking about what she already would have accomplished if she hadn't been stuck in a hospital bed. The woman had drive.

He eased into the chair beside her bed without releasing her hand. He'd hardly left her side since they'd brought her in last night. Even so, he'd been impressed with hospital security. When he'd spoken with them about the possibility of another attack, the EMTs had already relayed his message.

While she was still in the emergency room, one of the two officers who'd responded had taken her statement. Eventually, they had moved her to a private room, assuring him that her presence there would be kept confidential.

Kassie raised the back of the bed a little more. "Have you learned anything about the guy who attacked me?"

"Not much. He's refusing to talk. I would have loved to interview him, but I didn't feel comfortable leaving you." He gave her a teasing smile "Besides, I might have tried to wring the information out of him."

Kassie returned his smile. "I think he would have deserved it."

"We do know who he is now. The identification he carried was fake. All three pieces. But it didn't take long to get a match on his prints."

"You knew him?"

"Once I heard the name Louis Ballard, it all came back to me. I was a rookie cop when my partner and I arrested him for beating his girlfriend within an inch of her life. Several other charges got added to the battery charge, one of which was possession with intent to sell."

Sam had called him this morning with the same information, excited that one of the leads he followed had finally panned out. After the time his friend had put in, Jared almost felt bad telling him that they'd apprehended the man a few hours earlier.

Jared continued. "He's had warrants out for a while. Over the years, he's moved on to bigger and badder things. Now he's a midlevel dealer, buying small shipments of drugs and distributing them along the Gulf coast."

"Buying them from my dad." She heaved a sigh, shoulders slouching. Although she and her dad weren't close, learning about his illegal activities had obviously been a huge blow.

He squeezed her hand. "I'm sorry."

She looked up at him. "Why would he even get involved in something like that? He had the charter business, a beautiful home paid for, a daughter who adored him." She winced, as if she'd just noticed the word she'd used—*daughter* rather than *daughters*.

The soft tap of shoes against the vinyl floor drew his attention toward the doorway. A nurse walked in carrying a clipboard, a small stack of papers attached.

"Are you ready to get out of here?"

"I've been ready almost since I arrived." Kassie smiled. "No offense to you guys. Y'all have been great."

"No offense taken. Nobody books a stay in the hospital to get away for some R & R."

Soon the forms were signed and the nurse was wheeling Kassie through the hospital toward the main entrance. Jared hurried to bring the Suburban up under the covered area.

During the fifteen-minute drive home, Kassie stared out the front windshield, oddly quiet. He cast her several sideways glances before stopping at a red light.

"You okay?"

"I'm just thinking."

"Care to share?"

"I need to leave."

He looked over at her. "Where would you go?"

"I don't know, but my presence is putting your grandma in danger."

A horn blew behind him, and he stepped on the gas. "What would have happened if Justice and I hadn't been there last night?"

She heaved a sigh, her upper body deflating with the action. "I'd be locked up in a soundproof room…"

He finished her thought. "With a crazy man trying to not-so-gently coax information from you that you don't have."

A shudder shook her shoulders. The image they'd painted together didn't do much for his state of mind, either.

He pulled into his grandmother's driveway and killed the engine. "You're safest where you are—with Justice and me. When we're not there, you have no idea how often other officers and I are driving by to check on you."

She turned to look at him, features twisted in worry. "This isn't over. Eventually, the other guy will come after me. What if he's able to slip in without you and your cop buddies knowing and your grandma gets caught in the crossfire?"

"What if one of us gets hit by a train driving back from the grocery store?"

"There aren't any railroad tracks between the grocery store and here."

"My point is, no matter how careful we are, bad things can happen. Sometimes we have to do the best we can and trust God's protection for the rest."

She squeezed his hand. "Thank you."

"Let's go inside. Gram's been wound up so tight worrying about you, she's been in danger of snapping something."

That assessment got him a small smile. He stepped from the SUV and rushed around the front to help her from the passenger side. She was already sliding out when he got there.

"I'm all right. I'm pretty steady on my feet, in spite of getting punched in the head."

"Let me play the knight in shining armor, even if you're not the helpless maiden."

She put her hand in his and kept it there until they were inside the house. Gram sat in the upholstered chair watching some daytime television show, probably a soap opera, judging from the dramatic music and sappy lines.

Gram pushed herself to the front of the chair and hurried to stand.

Kassie lifted a hand. "Don't get up."

But Gram wouldn't be deterred. She gripped her walker and, when she'd made it to where Kassie stood, wrapped her in a tight hug, the walker between them.

Jared headed toward the kitchen. "Go ahead and take it easy. I'll make you some chicken noodle soup. Hopefully it'll make you feel better."

She looked around his grandmother, one eyebrow cocked. "That's for colds and stuff. I just got clomped on the head."

"Chicken noodle soup is good for whatever ails you—colds, flu, relationship problems, your favorite TV show being canceled…"

She giggled. "Actually, that sounds really good." She moved toward the kitchen with him. "I'll help you, though."

"I've got it if you need to rest."

"You're talking to somebody who's done nothing but rest for the past sixteen hours."

"You've got a point. You wanna cut up some celery and carrots?"

"Sure."

"We've got chicken left over from last night, so that part will be easy."

Once he had sautéed the veggies Kassie had diced, he added the cubed chicken, noodles, broth and seasonings.

Kassie leaned back against the counter and released a sigh.

"Is everything okay?" That sigh seemed to hold a lot of heaviness.

"I was thinking about Kris. She's not handling this situation with Dad very well. She was having a hard enough time coming to terms with his death. The thought that he was possibly involved in something illegal is about to break her."

He rinsed his hands and wiped them on a towel hanging from the oven handle. "She's had some serious bombshells dropped on her over the past few days. Have you two talked about it? She could probably use a sounding board."

"Until last night, we hadn't talked since finding the money in the house."

"That was several days ago." It seemed like a long time, especially under the circumstances.

"She had to work through her anger and needed time away from me to do that. Kris doesn't talk about what's bothering her until after she's had time to process it herself."

She heaved another sigh. "Finding the money was a shock to all of us, but you know what was the hardest? Seeing the pain on Kris's face. Even though she was trying to come up with other explanations, deep down she knew."

"So you talked to her last night."

"I called her from the hospital, told her about being attacked and that the guy was demanding I tell him where Dad is hiding."

"How did she react?"

"She didn't at first. There was just silence. I thought one of our phones had dropped the call. Finally, she said, 'I'm sorry.'"

"For what?"

Kassie shrugged. "For not believing me? For the times she lashed out at me when I tried to talk to her about it? For the threats I've received? Maybe all of the above."

She paused. "I told her I was sorry, too, for everything. We've had our differences, but we do love each other. Last night, she sounded so beaten down. I think this latest event was the straw that broke the camel's back. Except these aren't straws I've been dropping on her—they're logs—and the last one buried her."

He moved to stand in front of her and wrapped his arms around her. She didn't resist or even stiffen. Instead, her hands slid around his waist.

"It'll take time, but she'll get over it. She's got an amazing sister to help her through it."

She tightened her hold on him and nestled the side of her face against his throat. He closed his eyes, breathing in the faint fruity scent of her shampoo. It was the first time in two years that he'd held a woman like this, and he didn't want to let her go.

Contentment flowed through him. It started as heat in his stomach, building and spreading outward like warm honey, touching those places of his heart that he thought would never be warm again.

He was comforting her, but she was also comforting him, and it felt so right. It was time. This was what Miranda would have wanted, for him to let go of the grief, while holding onto the memories, and allow healing to begin in earnest.

Without releasing her, he pulled back just enough to look down at her. She tilted her face upward, her gaze searching his, her lips parted.

He lowered his head slowly, giving her the opportunity to turn away if this wasn't what she wanted.

She didn't.

When his lips met hers, he had no doubt. She returned his kiss, whatever reservations she may have had falling away.

The ringtone sounded on his phone, and he groaned. "It can go to voice mail."

"What if it's important?" She asked the question against his mouth.

"More important than this?"

"You'd better at least see who it is." She turned her face away.

He pulled his phone from his pocket, annoyed at whoever had the world's worst timing.

His annoyance dissolved instantly. It was Wayne Strickland again, the lead investigator on Miranda's hit-and-run case. Maybe they had identified the driver.

He swiped the screen and uttered a tense "Hello."

Over the next minute, details flowed through the phone almost faster than he was able to comprehend. He closed his eyes and listened.

Yes, they'd apprehended the suspect. He'd finally decided he wasn't going down alone and had spilled everything. He'd been hired to plant drugs at Jared's house, but before he could pull into the driveway, Jared's cruiser had moved down the road toward him. He'd turned around and hurried back toward the entrance of the subdivision. When he rounded a curve, a woman was suddenly in his headlight beams. He didn't mean to hit her, but he had drugs in the car and wasn't about to stop.

While Wayne talked, Jared paced the small kitchen. A cold block of ice settled in his gut. He didn't want to hear the answer to the question hovering on the tip of his tongue, but he asked it anyway.

"You said the suspect was hired to plant drugs. Did he say who hired him?"

There was a pause, a stretch of silence. Maybe Wayne was giving him time to prepare for the answer. It didn't help.

"Silas Beechum."

Jared's breath released in a rush. His former partner. Jared had ruined the man's life and career with his questions, so he'd tried to ruin Jared's by having drugs planted.

Kassie stood from the table, where she'd moved to give him some space. Now she approached to rest an encouraging hand on his shoulder. She was there and would support him through the fallout from the grenade that had just shattered his life.

He didn't deserve it. He didn't deserve *her*. His actions, though right at the time, had inadvertently caused Miranda's death.

He swallowed hard. "Thanks for letting me know."

When he had pocketed his phone, Kassie turned to face him. She didn't ask questions. She didn't pry. She simply wrapped him in her embrace and held him.

It was wrong. He couldn't take solace in Kassie's arms. Now or ever. How could he grab hold of happiness with Kassie when his wife had died because of him? He'd done what he'd thought was the honorable thing, and Miranda had paid the ultimate price.

He grasped her upper arms and held her away from him. "I'm sorry. I can't do this."

Confusion filled her eyes, overlaid with pain.

He spun and stalked from the kitchen and down the hall to his room. Trying to peel the scab off his greatest wound had been a big mistake. He'd pulled Kassie into his pain, and now he'd hurt her.

After closing the door, he sat on the edge of the bed his head in his hands. He'd thought he was ready. He wasn't. With that kiss, he'd crossed a line, one that would be hard to step back over.

But that was what he'd have to do. He'd let Kassie know how much he valued her friendship and hope he hadn't put a big rift between them with his actions this afternoon.

Kassie would forgive him. She wasn't the type to hold grudges. He'd recognized that in her relationship with her sister. Gram would be disappointed, but it was for the best.

He pulled a pillow onto his lap and sank his fist into it. If he was so determined to avoid a romantic relationship with her, why did he want so badly to kiss her again?

ELEVEN

Kassie stared into her bowl of soup, Ms. MaryAnn across from her. It was steaming fifteen minutes ago. Now it was moving toward lukewarm. Full of veggies and chunks of chicken, it was seasoned to perfection. Unfortunately, she wasn't in a frame of mind to appreciate it. Jared hadn't reappeared since he'd pushed her away and stalked to his room.

Ms. MaryAnn reached across the table to pat the back of her hand. "He'll come around. You're the first person to crack that shell around his heart. I think he's a little freaked out by that."

Kassie nodded. Ms. MaryAnn didn't know what had happened beyond the fact that the driver of the car that killed Miranda had been identified, someone had been hired to do something related to drugs, and it was somehow connected to Miranda's death. That was all Kassie knew, too.

What Ms. MaryAnn didn't know was that she'd let Jared kiss her. Not just let him, but eagerly returned his kiss. Fortunately, they'd been out of view of the chair she'd been sitting in. She hadn't peeked in on them, either. Stealth wasn't possible for someone reliant on a walker.

Kassie brought a spoonful of soup to her mouth. Definitely lukewarm. If she didn't get finished soon, she'd have to microwave it to make it palatable.

Ms. MaryAnn had asked her to let Jared know they were ready to eat. Kassie had refused. Jared had been the one to push *her* away, not the other way around. If he ever decided to let her back in, he'd have to make the first move. She wasn't about to put herself out there twice. So Ms. MaryAnn had invited him. He'd turned her down.

Kassie spooned up some more of her soup. "After lunch, I'm going to the charter office to get some more bookkeeping done." Kris had gone up earlier to process the paperwork for some customers going out with Buck this afternoon. Despite the threats against their lives, they still had a business to run.

Kassie had just finished the last bite when the creak of hinges drifted down the hall. A few seconds later, Jared stood in the doorway. The small smile he gave her looked forced. "How is the soup?"

"Good. It was great hot. It's even all right…not hot."

He moved closer and glanced into her bowl. "If you're not having seconds, would you mind walking with me?"

"No seconds." Firsts had been challenging enough.

She carried her bowl and spoon to the sink, then looked at Ms. MaryAnn, brows raised.

"You kids go ahead. I'll finish eating and wash our dishes."

When they stepped out the door, Jared locked his grandmother inside and moved down the driveway. "Is the park okay?" As soon as the words were out of his mouth, he winced. "I'm sorry, that was callous of me."

"The park is fine. I love this place, and I'm not going to let one incident change that."

As they walked down the concrete path toward the circular raised bed, Kassie tamped down a shudder. Jared needed to start talking soon, anything to distract her from the images flashing through her mind.

"I owe you an apology."

Yeah, he did, and she wasn't going to give him a pass.

He stuffed his hands in his pockets. "That phone call. I got some news that knocked the foundation from under me. Before I explain, though, I need to give you some background."

"Okay."

He motioned toward their left where a wrought iron swing hung from a metal arch. "Shall we sit?"

"Sure."

When they'd both eased onto the swing, he released a long, slow breath.

"Back when I started with Mobile, I was paired up with an officer by the name of Silas Beechum. He was in his midforties, took me under his wing as a rookie cop, even invited me for dinner with his wife and kids. A couple of years after I started, I asked to see some evidence we'd taken in to compare to another case. It wasn't there—had never been logged in. The same thing happened again a couple months later."

"He was holding stuff back."

"Yep. My questions caused an investigation to be opened."

"And he blamed you."

"I had to testify against him, with his wife and older son sitting there. It tore me up. The guy had been so good to me and taught me so much, even made me part of his family."

"I'm so sorry. That had to have been hard."

"What he did was wrong, and I couldn't cover for him, but it was still one of the hardest things I've ever done."

"I can't even imagine." She held back the comforting hug she wanted to give him. She'd tried it earlier and he'd pushed her away.

"Anyway, Beechum went to prison for eight years, got out two years ago."

Two years ago… Realization slammed into her. "Beechum hired the man who hit your wife. He was to plant drugs at your house in retaliation for your turning him in."

"Except his plan went awry, and Miranda paid with her life."

"Did he hit her intentionally?"

"No. I got home from my shift before he could plant the drugs. He was hurrying away, came around a corner and hit her."

"And you feel responsible." She didn't phrase it as a question. She didn't have to.

"Of course I feel responsible. If I had kept my mouth shut, Miranda would be alive today."

"What, turn a blind eye when someone's breaking the law? Your job is to uphold the law." She gave his shoulder a shake. "You did the right thing. You wouldn't have been able to live with yourself knowing one of your fellow officers was a dirty cop and you stayed silent. There's no way you could have foreseen what happened with your wife."

"I know that up here." He pointed to his head and then splayed his hand on his chest. "I just don't feel it here."

He rose to face her. "I like you a lot, Kassie. You're beautiful, talented, kindhearted, smart, fun and a bunch of other adjectives it would take me too long to recite. I thought I was ready for a relationship, and if I was, you're the one I'd choose. But I'm not."

She looked up at him, hopes sinking lower with every word. She was getting dumped before they'd even gotten started.

He sighed. "I want to remain friends, but if you don't, I understand."

She stood and took both of his hands in hers in a gesture she hoped he wouldn't misinterpret. "It's all right. I understand." She was trying to, anyway. "I'm fine with friendship."

What choice did she have? Ms. MaryAnn was one of her closest friends, and Jared was her grandson. They were even living under the same roof.

She released his hands. "We should head back. I'm supposed to be at the charter office, and you'd probably like to get some sleep before your shift tonight."

"Sleep sounds good. But I wish you'd put off your work there until we know you're out of danger."

"I can't. Kris is going to fight me on it, but we've got to get the place sold. To do that, I need to get the accounting in order." She gave him a reassuring smile. "Don't worry. Kris will be with me. If it'll make you feel any better, we'll even have Don come over and escort us to our cars."

Back inside the house, Jared finished off the soup while Kassie helped his grandmother clean up their lunch mess. When he'd finished, he said good-night and headed to his room.

Ms. MaryAnn turned to her as soon as they were alone. "Do you two have everything straightened out?"

"We do." Not the way the older woman would hope, but yeah, it was straightened out. No misunderstandings. "We're friends. That's all either of us planned on from the start."

Her face fell, and Kassie winced, a pang of guilt stabbing through her. But she wouldn't be doing Ms. MaryAnn any favors by building up her hopes, only to dash them later.

She wasn't going to do it to herself, either. From the start, she'd sensed that Jared had his guard up. But she'd lowered hers anyway and allowed herself to entertain fantasies.

She hung up the towel she'd used to dry the dishes and picked up her purse and keys. "I'm heading to the charter office. I should be back around six thirty." She could make it seven to avoid facing Jared, but that would be reckless. No, she'd handle the situation like an adult.

When she stepped into the charter office, Kris was sitting at the desk in the lobby, phone pressed to her ear. Kassie waved and walked down the hall to their dad's office. After hanging her purse over the back of the swivel chair, she sank into it.

Kris's voice drifted down the hall. She verified the time

and place and wished the caller farewell. A half minute later, she appeared in the open doorway.

"Two more people for tomorrow's charter. That makes it full."

"Good." As far as Kassie could tell, they were getting enough business to keep the bills paid. But she hadn't drawn anything for her time since her father disappeared, and she wouldn't until she had a better handle on the company's finances.

Kris crossed her arms and leaned against the jamb. "Business is pretty brisk."

"That's good." She knew where the conversation was headed and wasn't going to let her sister drag her into an argument.

"It should give us some decent income in the years to come." She wasn't letting Kassie's crisp answers deter her. "Especially if we come up with some good marketing ideas."

"Uh-huh." Ignoring her sister, Kassie opened the file folder in front of her. It held the bank statement and receipts for the next month of accounting on her to-do list.

"We've got two charters filled up for next week. One of them is a nature outing, a group of hobbyist photographers. We're known for our fishing charters, but this is a market we haven't even tapped." She smiled. "Getting back to coming in regularly has been good for me. I've needed to get active again. I'm just now realizing that."

Kassie looked up from her work. Kris did look better, more engaged with life. The sad, beaten-down woman on the phone last night seemed to have disappeared. Someone else stood in her place—someone with a cautious anticipation that good might be waiting around the corner. If getting involved in the business again was responsible for the change, how could Kassie take it away from her?

Kris uncrossed her arms and pushed herself away from the doorjamb. "On another topic, things are getting bad between Shannon and Carl."

"Are they going to split up?"

"I don't know. She hasn't said much about it, but they're fighting a lot. I feel like he resents my presence there, as if he thinks I'm the cause of the friction between them."

"What are you going to do?"

"I don't know. I don't think he'd hurt us, but what if I'm wrong? His animosity is so uncomfortable, I'd almost prefer to take my chances with a kidnapper."

Kassie shook her head. "That's not a good idea."

"I'm just kidding, sort of. I'm not taking risks with Gavin's and my safety, but I *am* returning home."

Kassie looked at her sharply. "What?"

"I've contracted with a private security company."

"Can you afford that?"

"I'm going to use some of Mark's life insurance money. A lot of it's still sitting in our savings account. One guy's already been caught. I'm hoping they'll get the other one soon so I won't have to put too much of a dent in those funds."

"What if the guy gets past the security person?"

"Security people."

"You're hiring more than one?"

"Two will be there from sundown to sunup. One will be there the rest of the time."

"Okay, what if he gets past the security people?"

"And what if Carl flips out and comes after me? I'm safer with the trained security specialists."

"Maybe." She still didn't like it. Even with two security guards, the house was too large.

Kris narrowed her eyes. "Are you all right?"

"I'm fine. Why?"

"Something seems off. My forever strong, do-whatever-I've-gotta-do sister seems distracted, maybe even a little depressed. I think it's more than this mess with Dad and what we're going to do with the business."

Kassie shrugged. "I've got a lot on my mind."

Kris studied her a moment longer. "Something happened with Jared." It was a statement, not a question.

"We're just friends. What can happen?"

Suddenly, understanding flitted across her face. "You've fallen for him."

"No, I haven't." She put her face in her hands and groaned. "Yes, I have."

"I don't blame you. What woman wouldn't be attracted to him? I mean, he's good-looking, kind, compassionate." Kris grinned. "He's really hot in that police uniform, a pistol attached to his side." She grew serious. "So tell me what happened."

Kassie looked up at her sister, now leaning forward, hands on the desk. They must have entered an alternate universe. Even growing up, they'd never had the kind of relationship where they shared secrets. The competition between them had been too fierce.

But here she was, considering laying it all out, and she couldn't think of a reason not to.

She sighed. "We were both sure that all we wanted was friendship. But we've been inching toward something more. This morning he kissed me, and I encouraged it."

Kris tilted her head to the side. "You admitted you've fallen for him, so why is that a problem?"

"He pushed me away." Shame bore down on her, the sting of rejection. "He said he wasn't ready."

"He pushed you away? That doesn't sound like Jared."

"There *is* more to the story." She relayed everything she'd learned, from the way he'd lost his wife to how he'd been a victim of revenge.

Kris sank onto the couch across from her. "Whoa, that's some heavy stuff. Maybe he needs time to process everything. He's not ready to move past friendship now, but what about the future?"

"I know. In the meantime, though, living with him and his grandmother won't be easy."

"I can imagine." Her eyes widened. "Hey, why don't you stay with me?"

"Jared would have a fit."

"As if you're safe there. I mean, look what happened last night."

"You've got a point."

"At my place, you'd have armed security watching over you every moment."

She leaned back in the chair. The idea had appeal. For the time being, she needed to put some distance between herself and Jared. Cuddling Gavin and loving on Bella would be therapeutic.

Kassie met her sister's gaze again. "So when is this move happening?"

"As soon as I leave here. Our stuff's already in the back of my SUV."

A slow smile crept up Kassie's face. "Plan on some company."

"Awesome!"

After Kris walked away, Kassie shook her head. When she'd left ten years ago, she'd sworn she'd never again live in that house. There was too much unhappiness associated with the place. *Never say never.*

She would finish out the afternoon at the charter office, maybe get through another month of accounting. Then she'd have dinner with Jared and his grandmother.

Once Jared left for his shift, she'd break it to Ms. MaryAnn that she was leaving. She'd give Jared the news over the phone. Better yet, by text. Yeah, she was a big chicken.

He wouldn't be happy. He'd argue that the house wasn't secure with anything less than a squadron of security people. There were too many windows, double French doors all the way across the back.

But how safe was she staying with Jared? She wasn't.

No matter where she went, safety was just an illusion.

Kassie sank onto the family room couch next to Kris. Gavin was stretched out on Kris's other side, Bella on the floor in front of them. The dog rested her head on Kassie's foot.

Throughout the house, the drapes were drawn, even on the French doors, completely closing off the view of outside. Kassie had left Ms. MaryAnn's at dusk, but by the time she'd gotten to Kris's, darkness had fallen fully.

That hadn't been a problem. One of the security people had met her before she'd even killed the Sorento's engine. Then he'd escorted her into the foyer, even helping her carry her things. She'd been impressed with him. He was probably early to mid-forties, competent, alert and sure of himself. He inspired trust and a sense of safety.

She hadn't met the other one but had been assured he was in the back, where he'd remain until morning. At that time, a single replacement would be sent for both of them.

Kris picked up the remote from the coffee table. "How about a movie?"

"That's perfect." It would provide a distraction.

Ms. MaryAnn had been disappointed to learn she was leaving. She'd also been concerned but couldn't dispute the fact that she'd be well-protected.

Kassie still hadn't texted Jared. The problem was, the text would probably generate a phone call, something she'd rather not deal with. Maybe she'd really take the coward's way out and let his grandma tell him in the morning.

Kris pressed the power button, and a couple of rows of

icons appeared on the screen. "What kind of movie are you in the mood for?"

"You pick."

"A romantic comedy?"

Kassie groaned. "Please, nothing with romance."

"Good point. Suspense is probably out of the question, too."

"Yeah. We've been living it for the past three weeks."

"*You* especially have. A drama?" She didn't wait for Kassie to answer. "Nah, we have too much of that, too." She paused. "How about a disaster movie? That ought to cheer you up."

"How do you figure that?"

"Anything we've got going on pales in comparison to an asteroid hitting the earth, plunging us into another ice age."

"Well, that puts everything in perspective."

A little voice at the other end of the couch cut into their discussion. "Seepin' Booty."

Kassie smiled. "*Sleeping Beauty* sounds like an excellent idea."

"Are you sure? There's romance, a handsome prince and a kiss."

"And they all live happily ever after." She grinned. "Let's do it."

Kris rose to search the shelf that held Gavin's DVDs, sliding an index finger across their back edges. "Here we go, *Sleeping Beauty.*"

Gavin squealed and sat up, feet bouncing. Bella lifted her head to see what the excitement was, then apparently decided it wasn't worth her attention and resumed her prior position. Once Kris had slid the movie into the DVD player, she eased down next to her son.

As the opening credits rolled, Kassie slid her sister a sideways glance. Her head was turned away, her eyes no doubt fixed on her son. She'd probably watched the movie with him enough times to have the lines memorized. Kassie knew quite a few herself.

She returned her gaze to the screen. Sitting side by side on the couch in the family home, she'd almost say it was like old times, except *old times* weren't that great. Certainly nothing she looked back on with fondness.

Maybe this was a new start. Over recent years, her relationship with Kris had gotten better. But it still didn't take much to throw them back into the old tug-of-war.

Tonight, there was no tug-of-war. It was one of the few times in her life when she'd felt unity with her sister. That didn't mean there'd be no more disagreements, even fights. Tonight, though, it didn't matter. Kassie had needed her twin and she'd come through for her.

Music started up nearby, competing with what flowed from the surround sound system. Kassie looked at the end table next to her. Her phone's screen was lit, a name across the center.

"Uh-oh."

Kris looked over at her. "Who is it?"

"Jared. I'm guessing his grandma decided to not wait till morning to break the news."

"Or he drove by and your car was gone."

Kassie winced. "I didn't think of that."

"Do you want me to pause the movie?"

"You guys go ahead. I'll talk to him in the kitchen."

She swiped to accept the call on her way out of the room. Jared didn't bother to return the greeting.

"Are you crazy?"

"No, I'm quite sane." She leaned back against the counter. "I'm inside with the doors locked, the alarm set and two armed security guards outside."

"Does this have anything to do with our exchange this afternoon?"

She opened her mouth to deny it but couldn't. She didn't

have to admit it, though. "Things were getting bad for Kris at Shannon's, so she hired security and came home. She invited me to stay with them, and I accepted the offer."

"So this is what you do."

"What do I do?"

"Things get a little uncomfortable between us so you take off, putting your life at risk, taking reckless chances."

Heat shot through her. "Are you forgetting that a little more than twenty-four hours ago, I was in the process of being abducted from your house?"

A heavy sigh came through the phone, as if her words had deflated both his argument and his anger.

She lowered her voice. "I'm as safe here as I was at your gram's. Safer since we're under surveillance 24/7."

A span of silence followed. Maybe he was letting her words sink in. Finally, he spoke. "You're right. I'm sorry I blew up. I prefer to keep you with me."

"Remember, I could get hit by a train."

"You're throwing my own analogy back in my face?"

"I am. Sometimes we have to do what we can and trust in God's protection for the rest."

"We're still going to have units drive by."

"Extra backup doesn't hurt. God doesn't need it, but the two guys outside probably won't mind."

His radio crackled in the background. "Hold on."

A few seconds later, he returned. "I've gotta go. Stay safe."

"I will."

When she returned to the family room, Gavin had lain down, his head resting in his mother's lap. Kassie stepped forward to peer at him. Although his eyes were still on the screen, his lids were at half-mast. With each blink, they took longer to open.

"He's falling asleep." She whispered the words.

"We'll head upstairs soon." Kris's tone was equally soft. "I'll put him down, then get ready myself."

"I'll probably read awhile before going up."

A few minutes later, Kris gently lifted her son's head and shoulders and slid from beneath him. Gavin drew in a breath and released it in a sigh but didn't stir.

"Come, Bella." She headed toward the French doors along the back wall. "Last chance to go out before morning."

The dog rose and padded across the room. As Kris unlocked one of the French doors, Kassie tensed, then shook off the uneasiness. One of the security people was out there, constantly watching the back of the house.

After Bella shot out the door, Kris lifted a hand to wave, confirming Kassie's silent pep talk. She waited a few minutes with the door closed, then reopened it and whistled for Bella. The dog came bounding back inside, tail wagging.

When she hit the power button on the remote, Gavin raised his head. "Seepin' Booty?"

"We'll finish watching *Sleeping Beauty* tomorrow night."

Kris picked him up and walked from the room, Bella following. A few seconds later, footfalls sounded on the steps—the hurried tread of the dog scurrying upward, claws scraping the hardwood surface, followed by Kris's slow, purposeful ones.

Now alone in the family room, Kassie picked up her reader from the coffee table and settled back on the couch. All was quiet except for the soft creaks made by Kris's footsteps. Soon, even those fell silent.

After reading for about twenty minutes, Kassie looked up, a chill passing through her. A faint metallic sound had come from the other side of the room. She fixed her gaze on the two sets of French doors that led out to the patio overlooking the bayou.

What had she heard? The jiggle of a doorknob? A creak of the old house? Probably nothing. She needed to keep a tighter rein on her imagination.

The next second, a crash wrenched a scream from her throat. One set of French doors exploded inward, setting off the alarm. Two men entered as she sprang to her feet. They were dressed in all black, from their knit ski masks down to their boots.

She snatched her phone from the end table and ran from the room. Her heart pounded out an erratic rhythm, more terror than exertion. If she could make it to the front door and outside, maybe a neighbor would hear the alarm and rush over to investigate.

She'd just reached the foyer when muscular arms wrapped around her midsection and threw her to the floor. She landed on one extended arm. Pain shot through her elbow and wrist.

She screamed again, loud and long. Kris was probably already calling the police. *Just don't come downstairs.*

The phone rang. Likely the company that monitored the alarm. If no one answered, they'd place a second call to the police.

One of the men forced her onto her back and, straddling her, held her shoulders against the floor. She twisted and bucked but couldn't free herself. He placed more and more of his weight on her until her hips and pelvis felt as if they'd crumble.

Her second assailant was only slightly smaller. When he wadded up a rag, she clenched her jaw and tossed her head side to side, until the first grabbed a fistful of her hair and gave it a firm yank. Her mouth snapped open in an involuntary cry. The next moment, the wadded-up rag went forcefully inside. It tasted of cigarette smoke and sweat and absorbed her screams.

Once they had her silenced, the man straddling her flipped her onto her stomach and wrenched the arm she'd landed on behind her back. Renewed pain shot from her hand all the way into her neck, as piercing as an electric shock.

Something metal clicked around her wrist. When a strong hand clasped her other arm, she tried to jerk it away. If she stalled for time, maybe help would arrive before they could take her away.

Pain shot through her shoulder as he wrenched her arm behind her. Metal clicked around that wrist, too. Definitely handcuffs. After tying her ankles together with a short length of rope, they wrapped a strip of cloth around the lower part of her face and secured it behind her head.

Two muffled barks came from upstairs, barely audible over the alarm. Kris was likely trying to keep Bella quiet and not alert the intruders to their presence. Kassie wouldn't either. Whatever it took, she had to keep the men from going upstairs.

She stopped fighting. Let them take her. Then they'd leave Kris and her little boy alone.

The man straddling her rose and picked her up, tossing her over his shoulder as easily as if she were one of Bella's thirty-pound bags of dog food. Then he followed the other man through the family room and out the damaged back doors.

She raised her head to look around. Where were the security people? There were two of them, highly trained.

Oh, God, please let them be okay. If the two men died while protecting them, how would she live with that?

Her assailants tromped through the back yard, veering left to take an angled path toward the water, the smaller man in the lead. Were they going to drown her? No, they needed her alive.

They continued on, paralleling the shore, guided only by the glow of a half moon and what little light reached them from the backs of the houses. She prayed for someone to wander onto one of the patios or decks, then retracted the prayer. The man who carried her was armed, a pistol tucked into a holster at his side. She didn't want innocent bystanders killed trying to save her.

Eventually, the shore bent at an almost ninety-degree angle, putting them heading in a somewhat westerly direction. A short distance ahead, Yates Avenue dead-ended near the water.

An older sedan was backed into the trees and underbrush at its edge, partially hidden from anyone who might venture past the last driveway.

The smaller man pulled a set of keys from his pocket. Instead of approaching one of the doors, he headed straight to the trunk.

Her pulse kicked into overdrive. *No, not the trunk.*

He opened the lid, and the larger man tossed her inside. She landed against the thinly padded floor with a thud, the spare tire pressed into her back. The lid slammed shut, casting her in darkness so thick it had weight. A heavy sense of claustrophobia swept through her and behind it a wave of sheer terror. Where were they taking her? How were they going to try to force her to talk?

Once they recognized she was of no value to them, what then?

The answer loomed over her, deadly and sure.

They were going to kill her.

TWELVE

Jared drove through the streets of Pensacola, ready for dispatch to break up the monotony. In the meantime, he remained alert, always on the lookout for anything suspicious. Justice rode in the back, tail thumping the seat every time Jared spoke.

He'd already driven past the Ashbaugh home. He'd made sure others would too. That was all he could do. He had to trust the security personnel to do their job and trust God to protect the women and child inside should they fail.

Finally, his radio crackled to life. A break and enter with a possible kidnapping.

His heart leaped into his throat and a sudden weakness filled his limbs. He drew in a stabilizing breath. Pensacola had a population of more than fifty thousand. The odds the call had anything to do with Kassie and Kris were low. With the presence of the security team, they were even lower.

Then the dispatcher recited the address, shattering every one of Jared's silent reassurances. It was Kris's.

After responding to dispatch, he turned on his lights and sirens and made a U-turn at the first opportunity. He hadn't gone far when his cell phone rang. He snatched it from where he'd left it in his console and glanced at the screen.

Kassie was calling. Relief flooded him, then died, crushed by sudden dread. If Kassie wasn't the one who was kidnapped, that meant Kris was. Or even Gavin.

He touched the screen to accept the call and pressed the phone to his ear. "Kassie, what's happening?"

The voice that came through the phone wasn't Kassie's. He didn't even recognize Kris's behind the hysteria.

"Jared, they've taken her." The words flowed out, tumbling over one another. "I was upstairs. I'd just put Gavin to bed, and they kicked in the door."

It was Kris. "Did you see what they were driving or which way they went?"

"No." A sob rose up in her throat. "I didn't see anything."

"I'm three minutes away. Stay put and I'll be right there."

Minutes later, he screeched to a halt behind Kassie's Sorento. Justice followed him to the door, and Kris met them holding Gavin. The golden retriever stood next to her, pressing her weight into the side of Kris's thigh. After the two dogs sniffed each other, Bella looked up at him. Her eyes seemed to hold a silent plea. Was she upset because Kris was? Or did she sense Kassie was in danger?

He followed Kris inside, to the large family room at the rear of the house. Two sets of French doors occupied the wall at the opposite end, one set wide open, each door partially torn from its hinges.

"Tell me everything you know."

"I was in my room when the alarm went off. I heard Kassie scream, so I locked the door and called 911." She shook her head, her face tortured. "I let them take her. I didn't come down and try to stop it."

Jared put both hands on her shoulders.

"You did the right thing. You protected yourself and your little boy."

A heavy knock reverberated through the house.

"More officers have arrived. We'll let them in and see if Bella can pick up a trail. Can you call Gavin's babysitter?"

"Yes. She lives a few doors down."

"Great." He took Gavin from her. The boy went without fuss. "Do that now."

He hurried to the front and filled the two officers in on what he knew. "There are supposed to be two security people watching the house. Someone needs to try to locate them."

"Will do."

The two men headed off in opposite directions, and he retrieved his flashlight from his cruiser. As he stepped back onto the porch, Kris appeared at the door.

"She's throwing on a robe and slippers and driving right over. I'm putting on some tennis shoes."

Jared nodded. She was dressed in jeans and a T-shirt. Maybe she'd only gotten as far as removing her shoes when the break-in happened.

It didn't take long for the two officers to report back. Both men were lying unconscious, apparently hit by tranquilizer darts. An ambulance was already on its way.

Jared stepped outside and paced the long porch, Gavin in his arms. Justice looked up at him, awaiting instructions. Jared didn't have any to give. He pointed to the space between two rocking chairs. "Lie down."

Finally, a vehicle pulled into the driveway, casting him in the glow of its headlights. A middle-aged woman jumped out and approached them at a full run. When she held out her hands, Gavin reached for her without hesitation.

Kris appeared, and the woman waved her away. "Go. I've got Gavin. I'll stay as long as you need me."

"Thanks. We'll start in the family room." She was already headed that way at a jog, Bella beside her. After giving Justice the command to come, Jared followed.

Kris stopped in the middle of the room. "Bella, search. Go find Kassie."

The dog sniffed the air and made her way to the door. Kris

walked behind her. Jared clicked on his flashlight and followed them into the night, Justice trotting beside him.

The trail made a diagonal path toward the water. Maybe the intruder took her away by boat. He gripped his radio, ready to relay anything they learned. *God, please help us find her.*

As they neared the left corner of the back yard, Jared swept the flashlight's beam back and forth ahead of them. No footprints marked the narrow strip of sand between the yard and the water's edge. Of course her abductors wouldn't leave tracks to follow.

Sure enough, a foot from where the yard ended, Bella took a sudden left, still sniffing. The search continued for another several minutes. Then the trail veered away from the water toward a thin patch of woods that bordered a house. The dog suddenly stopped her forward movement. She walked back and forth and made a couple of tight circles before sitting.

"What's she doing?"

"She lost the scent."

Jared studied the ground in the beam of his flashlight. A few feet from where he stood, tire tracks led away from them and disappeared at the road.

Kris gripped his upper arm. "They put her in the trunk." Her voice broke as she finished the observation.

Yeah, he'd noticed it, too. Kassie's scent ended a few feet behind and between where the tire tracks started.

He radioed in what they'd discovered. Detectives would already be on their way. They would photograph the tire tracks, maybe make castings.

It wasn't much to go on.

But it was all they had.

The whole world was rocking.

Kassie planted her feet in a wide stance to keep from falling off the bench and onto the floor. She had no idea where she was, just that she was on a boat, bouncing over the waves in open water.

The men had driven for about an hour before stopping. The final ten minutes had been on dirt riddled with tree roots and holes. She had no idea what direction they'd traveled.

When they'd opened the trunk and sat her up, she'd gotten a brief glimpse of her surroundings before they'd blindfolded her. There'd been woods all around, with total darkness except for bits of moonlight slanting through the canopy overhead.

After removing her from the trunk, they'd walked about twenty minutes before tossing her into some type of rowboat. A small motor had cranked up, and about twenty minutes later, they'd reached the boat they were currently on.

She was still gagged and blindfolded, but they'd unbound her feet so she could climb onto the larger boat. Though her wrists were cuffed, her hands were now in front of her. She'd at least be able to eat and take care of her personal needs.

She held a heavy chain gripped in one hand. The men had looped one end around the finer chain that connected her handcuffs and the other around the pole supporting the table in front of her. A padlock secured each end. She'd already checked it out.

Currently, she was alone, the men who'd kidnapped her on deck. There was a third, too. They'd spoken to him when they'd boarded with her.

The boat suddenly pitched, jamming her lower ribs into the edge of the table. She cried out, but the gag swallowed the sound. The volume of the engine dropped and the forward momentum decreased. The rocking became gentler and then stopped altogether. Maybe they were moving into a harbor or bayou.

Footfalls sounded outside. For the first time since they'd set out, voices were audible, too, although she couldn't make out the words.

When someone moved closer and tromped down the steps, her pulse jumped to triple time. Chained to the table, gagged and blindfolded, a sense of vulnerability overwhelmed her. Hot tears stung her eyes, and she squeezed her lids shut, trying to trap them inside.

Another man came down the steps, leaving just one driving the boat. From what she could tell, they were still moving, but barely, maybe preparing to drop anchor.

She steeled herself. For what, she didn't know. Were they going to hit her? Try to beat the information out of her? When hands touched the back of her head, a shudder shook her shoulders and rippled all the way down her back. The blindfold was snatched off, pulling her hair in the process.

Squinting in the bright light, she looked around her. She was in the cabin of a boat but didn't recognize the make. Outside the portholes, it was still dark.

Two men stood next to her. Judging from their size and clothing, they were the two who had abducted her. They still wore their ski masks. Since she wouldn't be able to identify them, maybe they'd let her go when this was over.

Not likely. She was dealing with bad men. None of them would have any qualms about snuffing out her life when they no longer needed her.

"Drake, remove her gag." It was the larger of the two who'd spoken.

The other man stepped closer—Drake, likely a nickname. "Don't bother screaming. No one's around for miles. You'll just tick us off. Understand?"

She nodded. He untied the gag and pulled the wadded-up cloth from her mouth. When she tried to moisten her lips, her tongue stuck to her gums.

"Can I have some water?"

"You give us what we want, and that'll be your reward."

She swallowed hard. She was going to get awfully thirsty.

"Let's start with where your father is hiding." Apparently, Drake was going to interrogate her. It didn't take him long to get started.

"I haven't heard from my father."

"Wrong answer." He looked at the big guy.

The open palm that slammed into the side of her face seemed to come out of nowhere. Her head snapped to the side, her neck making a sharp crack. Fire raged in her cheek.

"We'll try this again." Her interrogator wasn't through. "Where is your father?"

"His boat was found forty miles offshore, the dinghy still attached. Do you really think an almost sixty-year-old man could swim that distance without giving out or being dinner for a hungry shark?"

"Your argument's good, except for one thing. He was bringing back a shipment of drugs. If he'd fallen overboard, the drugs would still be on the boat."

"Then why can't you find another supplier and leave me out of it?"

"He has our money. His requirements were half up front, the other half on delivery. He kept our money and took off with our drugs." He dropped his voice, his tone low but lethal. "No one rips us off without someone paying. Ram here is good at extracting payment."

Drake sank down beside her on the long, curved bench. Mere inches separated them. He grabbed a handful of her hair and twisted it around his fist, each twist pulling it tighter. He tipped her head back until she was staring at the ceiling, then leaned so close his breath brushed her ear.

"I had a nice conversation with Alyssa. She said if her father would have contacted anyone, it would have been you."

Kassie didn't respond. That wasn't correct. Alyssa had said *sister* but hadn't specified which one. No matter what they did to her, the men would never know they'd taken the wrong sister.

"*If* he would have contacted anyone. He hasn't." She tried to look at him but couldn't turn her head. "How can you be sure he's alive? Let's say he did leave the boat with the drugs. Maybe he never made it to shore."

"He planned this out too well. He planted the bottles to make it look like he got drunk and fell overboard, but he'd already made arrangements for his escape."

"If that's true, do you think he's stupid enough to drag his daughters into it by making contact with us?"

He untangled his hand from her hair. "Don't worry, we've got ways of drawing him out."

He stood and dropped to his knees next to the table. Soon he'd removed the padlock securing the other end of the chain around the table pole.

He handed the links to the larger guy—Ram, definitely a nickname. Except for when he'd slapped her, he'd watched the entire exchange wearing a scowl, his arms crossed.

"Lock her in the head. After she spends a few hours in there, maybe she'll be ready to talk. If not, we go to plan B."

Plan B?

Ram slipped a hand under her armpit. After yanking her to her feet, he shoved her into the small room at the edge of the galley. An elliptical-shaped porthole occupied the space above and behind the toilet. Maybe daylight would offer a clue to her whereabouts.

Soon Ram had the other end of the chain looped around the shower grab bar and secured with the padlock. Then he stepped out and slammed the door, leaving her in darkness.

She sank onto the toilet lid, head lowered and shoulders drooping. No matter what they did to her, she couldn't give them information she didn't have.

If she could stall, she could give the authorities more time to locate her. But what leads did they have? As far as she knew, no one saw them carrying her along the shores of the bayou or stuffing her into the trunk of the car.

Maybe when morning came, someone would happen upon them and she'd be able to signal them through one of the portholes.

Not likely, but she had to hold onto something.

God, please get me out of this.

The gentle sound of lapping water seemed to come from all around, barely audible. Its soothing quality was deceptive, because something unsettling seemed to lurk somewhere close.

Kassie awoke with a start. She'd dozed off, sitting propped against the wall, the counter top pressing into the side of her arm.

This was her second time being chained up in the head. The first time, they'd left her sitting there for an hour or two. Then they'd freed the chain from the shower grab bar and hauled her back into the galley, asking if she was ready to cooperate.

When she'd repeated the answer that had gotten her slapped previously, she'd lifted her hands to try to deflect the blow. Instead, it had driven the edge of one of the metal handcuffs into her upper lip, putting a decent-size gash in it. Now it was swollen and stiff with dried blood.

She leaned against the counter. It had to be daylight, but she couldn't guess the time. While Ram had kept her seated at the table, Drake had taped a black plastic bag over the elliptical-shaped porthole.

Outside her tiny space, all was quiet. Maybe the men were taking turns sleeping, one stretched out in the front berth and one on the long bench seat in the galley. The third would likely be keeping watch. They'd probably all had at least one meal and several drinks since coming aboard.

Not her. She hadn't had anything to eat or drink since dinner last night. The thought of food turned her stomach. But she'd give anything for a glass of water.

She couldn't see the faucet, but it was there—tantalizingly close yet out of reach. Her thirst was only going to get worse. How long could one survive without water? Not nearly as long as one could survive without food.

She probably wouldn't have to worry about either. Once the men were done with her, they'd kill her. Unless she could find a way to escape. She would remain alert. Chained up, alone with three men, her situation looked hopeless. But as long as she had breath, she wouldn't give up.

The sound of footsteps reached her, at first distant, then moving closer. Someone seemed to be approaching from the front berth. She held her breath. Maybe they would cross through the galley and head up the companionway steps.

The movement stopped. Someone stood right outside. When the door handle clicked, her heart raced, sending blood roaring through her ears.

The door swung open, and light flooded the tiny space. Ram filled the opening. When he stepped closer, she tamped down an irrational urge to scramble away. Even if she weren't chained, there'd be nowhere to go.

Instead of touching her, he leaned over the bathtub and slipped a small key into the padlock. Once she was free, if she caught him off guard and toppled him head first into the tub, maybe she could run up top and jump overboard.

But there would still be two men to contend with and likely not a soul for miles. And she'd still be handcuffed. No, it was too early to act.

When he gripped her upper arms and jerked her to her feet, she stifled a scream. He dragged her, stumbling, from the bathroom and tossed her onto the bench seat so hard her head slammed into the wall behind her. The table she'd been chained to earlier had been removed.

Drake stood towering over her, arms crossed. "I haven't had any success in getting my questions answered."

"Because I don't know the answers. If I knew where he was, I'd tell you. I have no intention of willingly paying for his bad choices."

"I believe you."

Her jaw dropped as something like hope shot through her, but it was short-lived. If he believed her, he knew she couldn't help him. Had they brought her out to kill her?

God, please protect me.

"We've been calling and texting him, and he hasn't responded. We even let him know we have you."

He walked to the other end of the galley and back again before continuing.

"You know what we think? Old Man Ashbaugh isn't worried enough about his daughter yet. He needs a little motivation."

He gave his partner a nod. Before Kassie could even question what that meant, Ram's fist slammed into the side of her face, between her temple and eye socket. White hot pain exploded through her head.

The next blow came from the other side, connecting with her cheek. She was still reeling from the first two when an open hand caught her in the mouth, slicing the inside of her lip on her lower teeth.

Anger blended with pain and terror. Tears sprang up and overflowed, making rivulets down both cheeks.

Ram made a fist again, but before he could swing, Drake held up a hand. "That's probably good for now."

For now? Dear God, help me. How much more could she take?

Ram returned her to her prison, chaining her as he had previously. Over the next hour, her face throbbed, the skin growing tighter as the tissues beneath swelled. When he finally brought her back out, darkness had fallen. The only light in the cabin was what came from over the galley counter.

Drake held a phone. He flashed her a smile, but it held cruelty. "We're making a video and you've got the lead role."

He touched the screen a couple of times. "You're going to let your father know how important it is for him to listen to us. Think you can do that?"

She nodded, her mind racing. If only she could tip him off as to her location, or even what kind of boat she was on. But she didn't know either.

"If he doesn't respond to the text, we'll try some other options."

A sliver of hope shot through her. Maybe the video would wind up in the hands of the police. The more of the boat she could force the men to capture, the better the chances of someone identifying it.

That would be her only hope, because nothing the men could do to her would draw her father out. He'd sacrifice his freedom or even his life for Kris, but not for Kassie or Alyssa. Kassie had always reminded him of his unfaithful wife, if not her looks, then her musical ability and her personality. And he'd never believed Alyssa was his.

Her father wouldn't come for her. But she would let them make the video. She'd say whatever they wanted her to say. It would buy her time.

In the intervening hours, she'd pray with everything in her that the video would fall into the right hands.

THIRTEEN

Jared pulled from the station parking lot, ready to head home. His shift wasn't over yet. He wasn't even ready to call it a night. But his supervisor had insisted. He hadn't been to bed in thirty-six hours and was dead on his feet. When he got to Gram's, though, he probably still wouldn't sleep.

Time was ticking by far too quickly with no breaks. After twenty-four to forty-eight hours passed, the chances of finding abducted people alive dropped dramatically. Kassie hadn't been gone forty-eight hours yet. That wouldn't be until tonight. But she'd passed the twenty-four-hour mark five hours ago.

The suspect in custody still wasn't talking. The night Kassie was taken, while detectives had tried to lift prints inside and outside the house, taken pictures or casts of the tire tracks and handled everything else involved in the investigation, Jared had gone door-to-door talking with Kris's neighbors. None of the residents along Bayou Texar had happened to look out the backs of their houses to see anyone walking along the water's edge. And no one had heard anything.

He'd struck out everywhere he'd gone, except for one house, situated near the end of the dead-end street. Two neighbor kids had seen a car parked there, partially hidden in the trees. They'd identified it as an older Chevy Malibu, the 2008 to 2012 body style. Since then, the authorities had been checking out everyone in western Florida, as well as southern Alabama, Georgia and Mississippi, who owned a Malibu between those years.

The search had produced five possible matches within a 150-mile radius. They'd already eliminated four of them. One, though, belonged to a subject of interest. He lived in Atmore, Alabama, not far from Mobile, and was well-known to the authorities there, for everything from theft to possession to trafficking.

Jared pulled into the driveway and killed the engine. A dim light shone from Gram's room. At shortly after four a.m., she should be sound asleep. She was likely up praying, something she'd been doing almost nonstop since they'd learned of Kassie's abduction.

He turned to look in the back seat of his cruiser. "Come on, boy, let's try to get some sleep."

Justice lifted his head and whined. Maybe the dog was simply picking up on Jared's despair, but the way he'd been acting, he seemed to somehow know that Kassie was in danger.

As he stepped from his vehicle, his cell phone rang. His pulse kicked into high gear. *God, please let it be a break in Kassie's case.* He pulled the phone from his pocket and looked at the screen. *Kris?*

For her to be calling him at this time of the night, something must have happened. His hand shook as he swiped to accept the call. Panicked words tumbled out over the top of his "Hello."

"Kris, slow down. I can't understand you." He climbed back into his vehicle. "Are you at home?"

"Yes."

"I'm headed your way. Tell me what happened."

She took a deep breath, audible through the phone. "They sent Alyssa a video. She's hurt, Jared." She ended the sentence on a sob.

A boulder settled in Jared's gut. The kidnappers had hurt Kassie and made a video. Were they demanding a ransom?

He backed into the street. "Hang on. I'll be there in a few minutes."

When he pulled into Kris's driveway, light poured from several of the first-story windows. He grabbed his laptop and stepped from the cruiser. Justice stood on the seat, waiting for instruction. He held up a hand. "Stay." He'd see what Kris had, then decide how to proceed.

As soon as he climbed the porch steps, the door swung open. Kris stood in front of him, cell phone clutched in one hand, Bella next to her.

"Let me see what you've got."

She handed him the phone, where the video was already pulled up. He pressed the play button and an image filled the screen. It was blurred and there wasn't nearly enough light. But Jared had no doubt. He was looking at Kassie, and what he saw left a hollow void where his heart used to be.

Metal handcuffs restrained her wrists, a larger chain dangling from them. Her lip was busted and one eye was swollen almost shut. Her face had obviously taken more than one blow, and stains marked her shirt. He didn't need Hollywood quality video to know he was looking at blood.

As he watched, she swayed slowly side to side. She was apparently in a boat on open water, tossed by the waves. When she spoke, her voice was weak and her words were slurred.

"Daddy, please help me. If you can hear this, please listen to these men."

Jared clenched both fists. Her pleas shredded his heart. She'd fallen into the hands of some evil men. She was hurt and scared, and there was nothing he could do to comfort her.

The image switched from Kassie to a man dressed in a dark T-shirt and ski mask.

"Bobby Ashbaugh." He spoke in a harsh whisper. "Don't

let your daughter pay for your sins. You have twelve hours to return what you took. Involve the police, and she's dead. You know how to reach us."

Jared forwarded the video to his email. "Let's watch this on my computer and go through it frame by frame together."

Kris led him to the dining room, where they sat at the table and connected his laptop to her internet. Kassie was on a boat, but he had no idea what kind or where. The suspect in custody was known for distributing drugs along the Gulf coast, so his comrades who kidnapped Kassie were likely in something fast, like a cigarette boat, that would enable them to outrun the authorities. Or maybe they were in just the opposite—something unassuming where they could hide in plain sight.

Jared knew boats. He'd been around them all his life—both his grandfather's and several friends. Kris had, too. There were likely details on that video that they'd missed when viewing it on her phone.

They both leaned forward to peer more closely at the screen. His stomach clenched, and Kris released a small gasp. Kassie's injuries were even more evident.

He dragged his gaze from her face to look at the other details. The wall behind her was some kind of wood, maybe teak. He squinted at the images passing before him, searching for anything that could assist in locating her.

When the video ended, he played it again, and then a third time. Then he advanced through it slowly, frame by frame.

"They're not on open water."

Kris agreed. "Kassie's swaying, but the boat's still."

Maybe it was due to dizziness, possibly even a head injury. *Oh, God, please let her be okay.*

He continued his painstaking progress through the video. As Kassie swayed to her left, the camera caught the edge of a porthole. It was oval, or more accurately, elliptical. Not rectangular or round. That in itself would eliminate a certain percentage of boats.

There were other details, too. The bench she was on, as well as the wall above it, seemed to follow the curve of the boat. There was also no table in front of her. Either the table had been removed, or the boat featured a bench seat besides the seating in the galley area.

There was something above, too, barely captured in the top edge of the image when she sat up straight—some kind of soffit area or storage space, white rather than wood-covered.

Kris raised a hand. "Hold it."

He slid her a glance. The boat wasn't familiar to him, but apparently it was to her.

"I know this boat." Excitement filled her tone. "When I was in elementary school, a friend's parents had one. I used to go out with them sometimes on the weekends."

"What kind is it?"

Several seconds passed in silence as she held her lower lip between her teeth. "Phoenix…no, that's not it. Not Spartan. It's something Greek, like from Greek mythology." Another short span of silence, then a gasp. "Trojan!"

"A Trojan?" He'd never heard of the brand.

"Yes. I'll do some research and try to get you some more information."

"I will, too." But first he'd pass on what he had. The sooner someone got the information into the hands of the Coast Guard, the better.

They not only knew the make of the boat. They'd also narrowed down where to look—somewhere still, like a lake or bayou. They just had to figure out which one before it was too late.

During his and Kassie's exchange in the park, he'd messed up big-time. That couldn't be his last face-to-face conversation with her.

Please, God, protect her. Please give me the opportunity to tell her how I feel.

The men on the video had given Bobby Ashbaugh twelve hours.

That meant Kassie's time was running out.

Kassie lay stretched out in the front berth, comfortable except that the chain didn't allow her to roll onto her other side.

Shortly after recording the video last night, the men had brought her to the berth. They'd screwed a drawer shut, locked the chain through the handle and left her alone. This was much more comfortable than sleeping sitting up in the head. But she wasn't gullible enough to believe they'd made the change for her benefit. They'd probably gotten tired of having their only bathroom tied up.

Once they'd moved her, they'd even begun giving her small amounts of food and water. Although her stomach rumbled almost continually, she was at least getting something. She wouldn't pass out from hunger or die of dehydration.

Footsteps approached the door from outside, and her pulse kicked into high gear. The men hadn't beat her since bringing her to the berth. They'd even been patient with her requests to use the bathroom. Now it had to be nearing noon. That meant the twelve hours they'd given her father to respond were over.

The door swung open, and Drake stepped in. She glanced at his hands. A plate or bowl or even a bottle of water would mean she still had some time.

His hands were empty.

She pushed herself to a seated position on the edge of the bed. Ram wasn't with him, so it wasn't time for another beating.

She'd only seen the third man twice, when he'd been in the galley as she'd passed through. They called him Snapper.

He'd worn a ski mask, too. He usually stayed on deck, leaving Ram and Drake to deal with her.

Drake leaned against the wall and crossed his arms. "We haven't heard from your father."

No, she guessed not. The odds of him seeing the video were slim. The odds of him doing anything about it were nil.

"We even sent the video to your sister."

Her sister? Oh, Alyssa, not Kris. Hope sparked inside. If Alyssa saw the video, she would have sent it to Kris, who would have contacted Jared.

"No one rips us off and gets away with it. What do you think is fair?"

Her thoughts spun. Was he giving her an opportunity to try to talk him out of killing her? He'd never removed the ski mask. That had to be a good sign. She wouldn't be able to identify him if he let her go.

She drew in a shaky breath. "I don't know, but killing me isn't fair. I had nothing to do with this. I didn't know my father was even involved with you guys."

He shook his head. "Someone will have to pay. You're the one here. Your father thinks we won't do it. I'd say losing his daughter and knowing he could have stopped it is pretty good revenge."

Her heart threatened to pound out of her chest. What could she say? She had no way to convince the men they were better off leaving her alive, nothing to use as a bargaining chip.

Or maybe she did. Hope coursed through her with the thought.

"I have a suggestion. My father was wrong, but if you kill me, you'll still be out your drugs. How about I give you your money back?"

"We paid him $120,000. I seriously doubt you have that kind of money."

"My sister can get the money." If they went for it, she'd call

Alyssa. She didn't want to endanger her, but Alyssa was street-smart. If anyone could talk her way out of danger, she could.

He pulled a phone from his pocket and tossed it into her lap. "Go ahead and make the call. And keep it on speakerphone."

She'd suspected he was the one in charge. Since he didn't have to clear anything with his buddies, she was apparently right.

She punched in Alyssa's number with shaking fingers, then pressed the speaker icon. *God, please don't let this be a mistake.*

It rang once, twice, two more times. *Please answer.* It was a strange number. If Alyssa screened her calls, she'd have to leave a message.

At Alyssa's "Hello," Kassie's breath released in a rush.

"Alyssa, it's me."

"Kassie! Are you all right?"

"I'm all right for now, but I need you to do something. Dad didn't deliver these guys' drugs. They've agreed to let us return their deposit. I need you to pull $120,000 from Dad's stash of cash."

She held her breath, willing Alyssa to play along. Whatever Kris had told her, there was no way she knew about the discovery of the cash. Neither Kassie nor Kris had been willing to set themselves up for the relentless hounding that would have followed—the demands to pay out her one-third.

Alyssa responded after the briefest hesitation. "Okay, but I might need a little time to get it together."

Yep, street-smart. And a really good actress.

Alyssa continued. "How do I get back in touch with you? This number shows up as blocked."

Drake leaned toward the phone. "I'll call you in two hours."

"Four."

"Three. Be ready." He snatched the phone and ended the call.

Kassie breathed a sigh of relief. She had no idea whether

the police would release the money, but she'd bought herself some more time.

Maybe it would pay off. The video was likely in the hands of the authorities by now. They'd know she was on a boat. Maybe they'd even figured out what kind.

Drake walked from the room, and she lay back down on the bed.

Another few hours. That was all she was guaranteed.

God, please give the men who are searching success.

FOURTEEN

"You need to get some sleep."

Jared looked up at his grandmother from his crouch in front of the refrigerator. He'd just finished grocery shopping and was putting everything away. "I need to get back to the station."

"You're not the only one working on this, right?"

"Of course not." There were several agencies besides Pensacola, along with Coast Guard personnel.

Gram wheeled closer to put a hand on his shoulder. "You've hardly slept for the past two days."

He straightened to stand, which put him more than a head taller than his grandmother. The extra height didn't do him any good. Not with the way she was looking at him, like she wanted to turn him over her knee.

She reached around him to close the refrigerator door. "Go get some sleep." She made a shooing motion with both hands. "You won't be any good to Kassie or anybody else if you keel over from exhaustion."

He heaved a sigh. "Yes, ma'am." She was right. He really was exhausted. "I'll get some sleep."

Justice followed him back to his room, where he kicked off his shoes and stretched out on top of the comforter. He should probably trade his dress jeans and button-up shirt for something more comfortable. But he wouldn't be there long.

An hour. Two at the most. Then he'd get up, change into his uniform and head to the station.

He rested his hands on his abdomen, fingers intertwined. Only when he closed his eyes did he recognize how heavy they'd become. He'd just started to drift when a ringtone jarred him awake. Without sitting up, he reached for his phone.

The caller was Kris. Unfortunately, he didn't have any news for her. He swiped the screen, and her words spilled out before he could give his greeting. "Alyssa just got a call from Kassie."

He sat up and swung his feet off the bed in one smooth motion. "What?"

"Kassie called Alyssa from a blocked number. Her kidnappers are willing to make a trade—Kassie for $120,000, the money they supposedly paid him for the drugs he never delivered."

Jared's initial elation took a nosedive. This was what he had feared. Too many things could go wrong while exchanging a hostage for ransom money.

Kris continued. "Can we get back some of the money the police took? You guys could set up surveillance and move in once Kassie and Alyssa are safe."

"Is Alyssa willing to do this?"

"Believe it or not, she is. It makes me feel bad for all the times I called her selfish."

He nodded. If the Coast Guard was unable to find the boat, or if they found it but the men had moved her, a ransom scenario might be their only shot at getting Kassie back alive. The decision wasn't his to make, though.

"Let me relay this to those in charge. Don't call Alyssa until you hear from me."

"Will do."

He ended the call, but before he could place the next one, his phone rang again. This time it was his captain, James Manning. He swiped to accept the call. "What have you got?"

"A Coast Guard plane has located what they believe is the boat near the Alabama/Mississippi line. It's in a protected area of Grand Bay, right off the coast of the Wildlife Management Area."

Hope surged through him. He was familiar with the location. It was a couple of hours away by water, still and quiet. It had to be the same boat.

"Can they tell if anyone is on board?"

"One man was up on deck. We're not sure how many people are below."

Jared pressed his lips together. "I need to fill you in on something else. Right before you called, I heard from Kassie's twin. She'd just received a call from the younger sister who claimed Kassie had called her from a blocked number."

He relayed the substance of the conversation, expressing his own reservations.

"I agree. We've already got one life hanging in the balance. I'd rather not make it two."

"So what's the game plan?"

"First, the sister needs to put them off, say she needs twenty-four hours to get the money together. That'll hopefully keep them from doing anything rash and give us a chance to move in."

"I'm going."

"You're not part of this."

"With all due respect, I am. I have been since the beginning. I'm the one who discovered her after the first attack and have been one of the responding officers on several of the calls."

"We'll likely have a SWAT team handle the rescue, slipping in in canoes or kayaks in the early hours of tomorrow morning."

"Let me be there. I want to see this through to completion. Justice and I will work with whoever is heading up the operation and follow orders to a T. You know me. I have enough training and restraint to not do anything stupid."

James didn't approve the request, but he didn't deny it, either. "You call the sister. I'll let you know when the plan is ready to put in motion."

After ending the call, Jared filled in Kris and asked for Alyssa's number. "Let her know to expect a call from me in a few minutes, but don't give her any details." Since Alyssa was having direct contact with Kassie's abductors, the less she knew, the better.

When he finished the call with Kris, he waited five minutes before dialing the number she'd given him. The phone had barely started to ring when Alyssa answered. She'd apparently been holding it.

After a brief introduction, he got to the reason for his call. "We're working on something. When these guys call you back, tell them you need twenty-four hours to get the money together."

"I can do that." She paused. "Jared?"

Several seconds passed in silence. "Go ahead."

"I'll do whatever I have to to get her back. We haven't always… I've said some things…"

"I get it." Regrets. He was right there with her.

He ended the call and lay back down to wait for an update. He wouldn't sleep. Most of his fatigue had disappeared with the first words out of Kris's mouth. Whatever remained had fled with learning about the discovery of the boat. If he stayed in his room, though, it would satisfy Gram. She'd be convinced he was getting the rest he needed.

Gram. He couldn't leave her hanging. He pushed himself from the bed. She was almost as worried as he was. Besides, she was a real prayer warrior. Right now, Kassie needed all the prayer she could get.

If everything went as planned, chances were good that he'd see her before daybreak tomorrow.

Thank you, God.

The door to the front berth creaked open and Kassie pushed herself upright. Alyssa's three hours were probably up. There was no clock in the room, but there were two portholes that the men hadn't covered. Though she couldn't get near either of them where she was chained, she could distinguish between day and night. Judging from the angle of the light pouring in, the sun was almost halfway through its descent.

Drake stepped in and tossed the phone at her. "Call your sister, speakerphone again."

She punched in the number, hands shaking almost as much as before. This time Alyssa answered much more quickly.

"Did you get the money?"

"I need another twenty-four hours."

Uh-oh, that didn't sound good. Maybe they were having trouble getting the police to release it.

Drake stepped closer. "I already gave you three hours. I don't tolerate missed deadlines." His words held a lethal tone.

"Expecting me to get that kind of money together in three hours is unrealistic."

He crossed his arms. "You don't have it, do you?"

"Of course I have it. Half of it, anyway. More than half. I just need time to get the rest of it. His cousin in Atlanta has agreed to meet me halfway."

His cousin in Atlanta? Where was Alyssa coming up with this stuff? The guy was never going to buy it.

In the silence that followed, Alyssa heaved a sigh. "Oh, come on. You don't really expect him to keep that kind of money all in one place, do you?"

He didn't respond, so Alyssa continued. "Once I've collected the last of it and done a final count, I'll figure out the safest way to transport it." She paused. "Where am I going with it?"

"You'll get that on a need-to-know basis. Let's just say you'd better get your hands on a boat. I assume as the daughter of a charter captain that won't be a problem."

"Not at all."

"Just get the money. I'll call you at six tomorrow morning with instructions. If that $120,000 isn't in my hands before noon, your sister is dead."

"You seriously want this to happen in broad daylight? Hey, I'm okay with it. I'm just surprised you are."

He paused, apparently thinking. "We'll do the exchange around midnight."

"I figured you'd see it that way. Gotta go. I'm leaving for Auburn now."

"Auburn?"

"Meeting Dad's cousin. He's a ways north of Atlanta, so Auburn is the halfway point." She paused. "Kassie?"

"Yes?"

"You're okay, right? They're not hurting you?"

"No, I'm fine." At least they hadn't hurt her since chaining her in the berth.

"Good." The next words were obviously for her captor. "I'm going to talk to her each time I talk to you, right up until we make the trade. If you hurt her, the deal is off. I put that whole $120,000 right back in all its hidey spots. Understand?"

Drake disconnected the call without responding. They could still kill her, but what Alyssa was trying to do was nice.

Kassie knew Alyssa was cunning, but she'd never realized she was so good at thinking on her feet. Their dad didn't have a cousin in Atlanta. And he certainly didn't have money stashed all over the southeastern United States.

But her stall tactics had worked. She'd demanded another twenty-four hours and had gotten it.

She couldn't stall indefinitely, though. Eventually, she was going to have to get her hands on $120,000.

Drake crossed the room. As he opened the door, his phone rang in his hand. "Well, well, well. Look who we have here."

The door swung shut.

Who? She stepped as close to the door as the chain would allow. His voice drifted to her, but the words were inaudible. The thump of feet followed as he climbed the companionway steps. Then there was nothing except the lap of water against the hull of the boat and the distant cries of sea gulls.

The rest of the afternoon and evening crept forward at a snail's pace. Dinner consisted of a small can of Beanee Weenee with a bottle of water. At one point, the motor on the rowboat cranked up, the sound gradually fading. Someone had apparently gotten tired of being cooped up on the boat and had made a trip to shore. He still hadn't returned.

Kassie couldn't see the moon from where she was chained, but it was apparently full or close to it. Outside the two portholes, there were periods of increased light, interspersed with shifting shadows as clouds drifted overhead.

What was Jared doing? Were Kris and Gavin in bed, or was Kris pacing the floor, wringing her hands? If Gavin was still up, was he crying to see his aunt Kassie?

A sudden sense of homesickness welled up inside, almost overwhelming her. *God, please let me see my family again. Please let me see Jared again. I want to go home.*

She closed her eyes against the tears that threatened, and then rolled onto her side. She needed to shut down the hopeless thoughts and go to sleep.

A short time later, a distant rumble of a motor reached her, and she sat up. It was probably just one of her captors returning. The odds of someone coming to rescue her were slim.

As the vessel approached, the roar of the motor grew louder, then abruptly died. The boat tilted. Someone had just boarded. When it tilted again, she stiffened. Had a second person boarded? Maybe two had gone to shore, leaving just one to guard her.

She stood, straining to see out the portholes a few feet away. Water surrounded her, gentle ripples marring its surface, a jagged streak of silver moonlight stretching toward the shore. In both directions, trees marked the horizon.

Sounds of activity reached her—movement, voices, footsteps descending the stairs. The voices were louder now.

"Where is she? I demand to see her."

Kassie's mouth fell open. *Dad?*

"You're not in any position to make demands."

A thud followed, like a fist making contact with a body. The responding grunt confirmed what she thought she'd heard. The blows continued, and Kassie pressed her fingers against her ears. It didn't help. Tears squeezed past her closed eyelids.

Maybe her father deserved what he was getting. He'd stolen from these men and put his whole family in danger. But listening to the thuds of their fists and his grunts of pain was more than she could handle.

Finally, a larger thump told her he'd collapsed to the floor. Even then the blows didn't end. They were likely kicking him. *God, please make them stop.*

Everything fell silent, and she dropped her hands from her ears.

"We're not done yet." As far as she could tell, it was Ram who spoke. He was probably the one meting out the punishment.

"I'm here." Her dad's voice was thin, strained. "So let my daughter go."

"Not so fast."

"We had a deal." He sounded as if he was having trouble breathing. "It's the only reason I came. My life for my daughter's."

"Speaking of deals, we had another deal. We give you our

money and you bring back our shipment. What happened to that deal?" Anger laced the words.

Another kick followed, ending in a high-pitched scream.

Kassie shook her head side to side. *No, no, no.*

"I wanted out."

"So you said."

"I knew the only way you'd let me out was if I was dead."

"Don't worry, you'll get your wish. But we have a few other things in store first."

There was some rustling, and her father cried out again. Then something was being dragged across the floor. The door to the front berth swung open.

Drake and Ram stood on either side of her father, holding him up. His head was tipped forward, his chin resting on his chest. His breathing was jagged and shallow. He likely had broken ribs. Internal injuries, too.

They turned and sidestepped to drag him through the doorway, then threw him roughly onto the bed. His arms were under him, tied together at his back.

When their captors reached the doorway, her father raised his head. "Let Kassie go. Please."

The return answer was just as soft but held an edge of cold cruelty.

"Not yet. There's one more guest coming to this party."

Kassie's heart sank like a boulder. Alyssa. She'd hoped to save herself and had brought her younger sister into the mess. Why did she have to make that phone call?

Now all three of them were going to die.

FIFTEEN

Kassie sat on the bed looking at the unmoving mass beside her. The room was dark except for the glow of the moon drifting in through the portholes. But she didn't need daylight to know her father was badly injured. Other than tying his hands behind his back, the men hadn't restrained him. He'd been beaten too badly to be a threat.

She was still trying to come to grips with his selfless act of love. Had he been mistaken about which daughter the men had?

Not if he saw the video. With her hair tumbling around her face, he'd have known he wasn't looking at Kris. Kassie couldn't deny it—her father was willingly giving up his life for her.

"Dad?"

He opened one eye. The other was already swelling. "I'm so sorry." His apology came through bleeding lips.

"How did you find me?"

"They texted me the video, said they'd kill you if I didn't respond." He paused to catch his breath. "I've made a whole slew of bad decisions in my life, but this was one of the worst."

The pain on his face was no longer just physical. "All your mother wanted was for me to quit drinking. I tried but just couldn't do it. I thought if I could buy her nice things, it would help make up for all the ways I'd failed her."

Kassie sighed, pain and regret weaving through her. "And she left anyway."

He flinched as if she'd struck him. "You're right. It was all for nothing. I tried to get out, but they wouldn't let me go. Once they had their claws into me, I couldn't get out unless I was dead."

"So you pretended to drown."

"I got a half mile from shore, pointed the boat into the Gulf with the throttle set on low and jumped overboard. I figured between the liquor bottles and beer cans, and given my history, no one would question what happened."

"It might have worked if you hadn't stolen their drugs."

"I didn't steal them. I threw them overboard."

Kassie's mouth dropped. "Did you really think these men wouldn't come after $240,000 worth of drugs or the $120,000 down payment they'd already given you?"

"I figured if they did, they'd assume the authorities discovered them." He heaved a sigh. "I see now how unrealistic that was, but I didn't want to risk the boat being impounded. I wanted to leave you girls the charter business, but it's not much good without its most popular boat."

It's not much good if we're dead, either. She curled her hands into fists. It was going to take her more than twenty-four hours to let go of her anger toward her father.

Unfortunately, twenty-four hours was likely all she had.

God, forgive me for my attitude. Help me make things right while I still have time.

"I've been a terrible father, to both you and Alyssa. I'm so sorry."

He turned his head away from her, his shoulders shaking with his tears. Seeing him so broken softened her heart just a little. But she had no words of comfort. She couldn't say it was all right, because it wasn't. And she couldn't downplay the years of disapproval, because she was still dealing with the fallout.

Much later, she lay listening to her father's even breathing.

Judging from the silence that hung over the boat, at least two of the men were asleep. There was no conversation, no movement that she could detect. But the quiet didn't help her sleep.

Twenty-four hours. That was all she had. Tomorrow Drake would call Alyssa to make the arrangements for her to bring the cash. She'd dragged her little sister into this. It was up to her to save her. Drake wouldn't trust her with the phone, but when Alyssa demanded to talk to her, she could blurt out a warning. Her punishment would be severe. But she'd handle it. Anything to keep Alyssa from coming.

She rose from the bed to look out the nearest porthole, three feet away. The scene outside shifted slowly as the boat swung on its anchor. It came to a stop, then drifted back again.

Kassie's breath hitched. Had she seen movement against the marsh grasses? She waited for the boat to swing back around.

Now she had no doubt. A canoe or kayak was slipping silently through the water. She held her breath as another one came into view. If they were sent to rescue her, when they tried to board, her kidnappers would kill both her and her father.

Her chances would be better if she wasn't trapped in the berth. And the odds of two against three were much better than one against three.

"Dad," she whispered. "Wake up."

He didn't move.

She couldn't talk any louder or she'd wake up their captors. With her hands chained, she couldn't even reach over to shake him awake. She lifted one leg to rest her foot against his shoulder and gave him a good shake. "Dad, wake up."

He moaned softly, and his eyes opened.

"There's someone out there." She glanced toward the porthole.

He lifted his head, suddenly alert. "Who?"

"I don't know. Two people in kayaks or canoes. This time of night, I don't think they're pleasure boaters."

"What can we do?"

"I want to untie your hands. Can you make it over here?"

"I'll try."

He struggled to sit up, breath hissing through his teeth. Between the injuries he'd sustained and being unable to use his arms, every step was a struggle, but he finally reached her.

While she worked on the knots, he stood leaning forward and to one side, his pain obvious with every gasping breath.

Soon she handed him the short length of rope. "Now, get back in bed, just like you were."

"What about you?"

"I'll get one of the guys to unchain me so I can use the bathroom." As he circled the bed, she looked around the space. There was nothing he could use as a weapon.

She watched him lie back down, hands behind him and rope hidden. "I don't know what's going to happen, so once I walk out of here, be ready to act."

She rapped on the side wall of the berth. "Drake, Ram. Are you awake?" She would take either. Hopefully not both. Snapper was likely on deck or in the pilothouse. Maybe he was asleep since there hadn't been any movement in some time. If two out of three of them were conked out, it would be easier to catch them by surprise.

She knocked again. "I need to use the bathroom."

Finally, the boat rocked slightly and footsteps approached. The door opened, and Drake stepped into the space, radiating annoyance. "Can't you wait till morning?"

"I really can't."

He walked away and returned moments later with the small key. As he opened the padlock, he looked over at her father.

Kassie followed his gaze. Her dad lay perfectly still, chest rising and falling with his even breathing. Nothing looked amiss.

Apparently satisfied, Drake led her from the berth. When

she walked through the galley, Ram was passed out on the bench seat, snoring softly. She tiptoed past him, the loose end of the chain clutched in one hand.

As soon as she slipped into the head and closed the door, she peered out the porthole. With her face pressed against the Plexiglas, she had a wide-angle view of outside.

She scanned the water right to left and had to stifle a gasp. A canoe moved silently toward them. Its occupant was dressed in all black, a helmet protecting his head and likely a bulletproof vest around his torso. An oar occupied his hands. Though she couldn't see them, there were probably some serious weapons on the floor of the canoe.

The second one was no longer visible. Maybe it was approaching from the other side. *God, please keep their presence secret as long as possible.*

She watched the first one slip silently toward the stern until it disappeared from sight. Then she flushed the toilet and stepped from the head.

Drake stood in the galley area, arms crossed, waiting for her to return to the berth. Instead, she took a step toward the open companionway door.

"It's pretty out tonight." She spoke softly. "I love looking at the night sky—the stars and moon." She took another step.

Snapper was in the pilothouse stretched out on the bench seat, one foot and lower leg visible. If she caught Drake by surprise, could she make it past Snapper before he awoke and recovered his wits enough to shoot at her?

"No stargazing tonight." Drake's tone was stern. "Go back to bed."

The boat shifted almost imperceptibly, and she tensed.

"What the…" Drake's question trailed off.

She had to act quickly. She gripped the chain about a foot from the bottom, lifted her hands and spun, releasing the heavy links as she did.

The chain connected solidly, but she didn't see where. Both the *thunk* and Drake's curses followed her up the companion-way steps. As she ran through the pilothouse, Snapper sat up and grabbed the pistol lying on the floor next to him, but it was Drake's footsteps that pounded behind her.

She scrambled onto one of the seats, but before she could jump overboard, Drake snatched her hair and yanked her backward. She released a shriek and struggled to regain her footing. If someone had boarded, they'd done it from the bow, because, except for Drake, she was alone in the cockpit. Clouds obscured the moon, casting everything in shadow. A crash sounded below, followed by the sounds of a scuffle. *Dad?*

Strong arms wrapped around her and spun her toward the pilothouse. Snapper stood in the opening facing them, pistol raised. Movement beyond him drew her gaze, and her heart leaped into her throat. Two crouched figures were creeping toward her from the bow, one on each side. Both were dressed in black, weapons poised and ready to fire.

Suddenly Drake swung her around in front of him, using her as a shield. A shot rang out, wrenching another scream from her. Drake's hold on her loosened, and he crumpled against her, his weight threatening to topple her forward. When she looked up, Snapper was standing over her, weapon still drawn. Instead of shooting her, he lifted the pistol to aim at a point behind her.

Two more shots sounded almost simultaneously. Snapper dropped to his knees. As Kassie scrambled to her feet, the barrel of his weapon followed her. He'd been hit. His face was twisted in pain. Something else, too. Rage.

Without hesitation, she leaped onto the seat and sailed over the side of the boat, casting a glance toward the stern. A third rescuer had come aboard, likely the one who had taken out Drake. *Jared?* Three more shots pierced the silence in rapid succession.

The next instant, dark water swallowed her. Staying submerged, she tried to propel herself away from the boat with furious kicks. Cuffed together and weighted by the chain, her arms were of little use.

When she could hold her breath no longer, she brought her body upright and kicked with all her might. Ten seconds passed, fifteen. How deep had she gone?

The chain was too heavy. It was pulling her down. She doubled her efforts, head tipped back, feet working until her leg muscles screamed.

Her face broke the surface. She sucked in a panicked breath and twisted to look at the boat. Ram was stepping from the cabin into the pilothouse, hands raised, while the two figures in black stood with their rifles pointed in his direction. Neither Snapper nor Drake was visible, likely both dead on the floor of the boat. Jared stood where she had gone overboard, staring into the water. Before she could call out, the weight of the chain dragged her back under. She fought to again break the surface, but no matter how hard she tried, life-sustaining air remained out of reach. Her lungs were on fire, the urge to inhale almost uncontrollable.

No, no, no.

She'd survived kidnapping, only to succumb to drowning.

Jared moved through the water, powerful strokes propelling him forward. He'd seen Kassie dive overboard and had stood watching, waiting to see where she would surface. The others had the situation on the boat under control. Two more had boarded after he had. Others were on shore waiting among the trees and marsh grasses holding high-powered rifles with scopes. Justice was with them.

He stopped swimming and looked around him. He had to be close to where he'd seen Kassie surface, but that had been more than a half minute ago. Where was she?

She'd been restrained, her hands tied or maybe cuffed. Hanging between them was what looked like some heavy-duty chain. She had managed her own rescue, but now she was in trouble.

He scanned the surface of the water, searching for any signs of movement. Panic threatened to overwhelm him. He had to stay calm, keep his head. Kassie's life depended on it. *Come on, Kassie. Where are you?* She had to be close.

After drawing in a deep breath, he submerged himself and turned in a slow 360. The world around him was inky black, fading to gray nearer the surface. If she was very deep, finding her would be almost impossible. *God, please help me.* He couldn't come this close only to lose her.

He swam in a large circle, arms moving in wide arcs. Finally, his fingertips brushed something. He stretched out his hand again, and tightened his fist around clothing.

When he broke the surface with her, he glanced at the boat. "Help me."

Kassie was unconscious and didn't seem to be breathing. He pressed two fingers to her throat and found a faint pulse. He needed to extract the water and get some air into her lungs.

He hollered for help again, but one of the SWAT members on the boat had already removed his tactical gear and was preparing to jump into the water. He was at Jared's side within seconds.

"Help me support her." He pinched her nose and breathed air into her lungs. Her chest rose and fell. Chest compressions were impossible.

Oh, God, help us. They had to expel the water. Maybe they could lift her and beat on her back.

He forced another breath into her lungs. Suddenly, she curled up as a coughing spasm overtook her. Water spewed from her mouth, and she opened her eyes.

Her lips moved. No sound came out, but he was pretty sure she'd just said his name.

"Let's get her to shore." The suggestion had come from the other man. "Can you handle her? If so, I'll bring both of our canoes in."

Jared looked at Kassie. "Can you make it if I take the weight of the chain?"

"I think so." Her voice was hoarse, and the words induced another series of coughs.

She wouldn't have to swim far—thirty or forty feet. Then she'd be able to touch the bottom and wade in.

A commotion erupted on shore. Justice was running full speed along the curved shoreline, several SWAT team members in his wake. When Jared glanced over at the boat, the man he'd seen surrendering several minutes earlier was gone. Lights had come on inside the cabin, illuminating the oval portholes.

Jared tested the depth of the water. "I can touch." He took Kassie's hands and pulled her along, holding her shoulders and head above the surface. Justice disappeared around the point of the shoreline. An agonized scream moments later told Jared that his dog had apprehended the third man and hadn't tried to be gentle.

After a few more glances, he identified the dancing glow behind the portholes. The third man had set the cabin on fire before coming up top and surrendering. He was destroying evidence. It didn't matter. Whatever was gone, he would go down for kidnapping.

Kassie recognized the eerie glow, too. "Fire!" The word was hoarse and shrill at the same time, her voice cracking at the end. "My father!"

What was she talking about? "Your father is on the boat?"

"Yes, in the front berth, maybe the galley."

Before he could call out what he'd learned, two SWAT

members emerged from the cabin and walked through the pilothouse carrying a third man. Someone else was still below. The flickering light dimmed and then disappeared altogether. A final SWAT guy followed the others onto the deck holding what might have been a fire extinguisher.

The roar of a marine engine drifted toward them, and Kassie looked around, eyes wide with panic.

"It's the Coast Guard boat. They've been waiting nearby."

Jared stumbled from the water with her to recline on the beach. A few yards away, the man who had helped him with Kassie pulled the first of the canoes onto the sand.

Jared drew Kassie into his arms, unconcerned with what the others might think. He'd almost lost her, but God had answered his prayer. He was being given another chance.

He stroked her face with his fingertips, his touch feather-light. Too many unsaid words were burning a hole in his heart.

"I'm so sorry I pushed you away. You've dealt with a lot of rejection, so I can only imagine how what I did hurt you."

He heaved a sigh, trying to figure out how to express what he felt without sounding as if he was making excuses. "I felt responsible for Miranda's death. I didn't feel it was fair for me to enjoy love with you when she'd had her life snatched away. But I know now, she would have wanted me to find happiness again."

She looked up at him in the moonlight, a soft smile creeping up her cheeks. "I understand."

Relief slid through him. She was so sweet, so gracious. "Miranda would have loved you." He grinned. "And Justice has right from the start."

"Where is he?"

"Taking down bad guys, at least one of them."

He looked up to see his dog loping toward them, feet kicking up sand. Moments later, he plopped down next to Kassie and whined, body quivering with excitement.

"Justice!" She lifted her hands, still cuffed, and cupped the dog's face.

When she dropped her hands, Jared drew her toward him and brushed her lips with his, ever so gently. "It's going to be hard for me to compete with my dog, but I love you and I hope you'll let me be your biggest cheerleader."

"I love you, too. I've been fighting it, but your Gram has seen right through me."

"She's going to be thrilled. You know, from now till the end of time, she's going to take the credit for what's happened between us."

"Sounds like you're planning to make this a long-term thing."

"You'd better believe it."

He looked beyond her to the spotlights moving toward them on the water. He would ask one of the others to take care of his canoe so he could return with her on the Coast Guard boat. An ambulance would be waiting when they returned. He'd even see if he could accompany her in that.

Because now that he had her in his arms, he wasn't going to let anything tear her from his side.

EPILOGUE

The MasterCraft cut a path through the waves, sending water spraying back from each side of the bow. Jared sat in the captain's chair, throttle wide open.

Kassie occupied the bench seat nearby, Justice stretched out on the vinyl cushion, his head in her lap. As she twirled her fingers in his fur, her ponytail whipped side to side. She closed her eyes, a sense of contentment flowing through her.

Three months had passed since her kidnapping. Neither Drake nor Snapper had survived their gunshot wounds. Ram had made it out of the ordeal alive but wouldn't be seeing freedom anytime in the next decade. Neither would the man they'd apprehended in the park. Ram had had numerous warrants out for crimes from drug trafficking to murder. The man they'd nabbed in the park had a rap sheet almost as lengthy.

All four had worked independently of any cartels, so there was no one else to come after her. Although that had provided her with an immediate sense of relief, it hadn't yet fully sunk into her subconscious.

She was getting there, though. The nightmares had decreased in number and she no longer found herself looking over her shoulder. She was almost back to taking the creaks of her house in stride instead of reaching for her phone, ready to dial 911.

Her father had survived the fire, as well as a gunshot wound to the shoulder when he'd kept Ram from going after her.

The authorities had charged him with drug trafficking, but he would likely receive a reduced sentence in exchange for testifying against the other men.

"How about some lunch?"

Kassie opened her eyes, and Justice released a bark.

"Hey, Bozo, I wasn't talking to you."

Kassie smiled. "I think we're both ready."

Jared guided the boat into the wide channel between Fort McRee and Fort Pickens, headed for the somewhat calmer waters of Pensacola Bay. After rounding a few bends, he dropped anchor off the coast of the Naval Live Oaks nature preserve.

He killed the engine and moved to the bow where he'd stowed the cooler. The first item to come out was a plastic container of dog food.

Justice lifted his head from Kassie's lap to stare at what Jared held.

"How does he know what's in there?"

"I've decided he knows more than we think he does."

She extended her arm. "Hand me the container."

When Jared complied, she took off the lid and walked to the stern. Justice followed.

"There you go, boy." She straightened and smiled at Jared. "Now I'll be his best bud."

"You're already his best bud."

Yeah, the dog had definitely gotten attached to her.

Leaving him to his lunch, she returned to her seat and removed paper plates and disposable utensils from a zippered bag.

Jared walked toward her carrying three plastic containers. "Fried chicken, potato salad and baked beans."

When he laid them out and removed the lids, she eyed the potato salad. "Mmm, that looks homemade."

"It is. I'd take the credit for it, but this is Gram's contribution."

Soon they had the food dished up and blessed.

Kassie picked up a drumstick and bit into it. "Guess who I heard from last night."

"Who?"

"Alyssa."

"She's averaging, what, about once a month?"

"Yeah. What's really amazing is that every time she's called, she's asked me how I'm doing and really wanted to know. And she *hasn't* asked for money."

"I think almost losing you shook her up."

"Either that, or she figures since Dad's not dead, it's too early for an inheritance." She winced. "I shouldn't say that. I mean, she was willing to bring ransom money to secure my freedom. I really owe her for that."

"See, your family isn't as dysfunctional as you thought."

"I guess not." She wiped her hands on her napkin. "Too many years of experience has trained me to always expect the worst from her. Old attitudes die hard." She picked up her fork. "Like with my dad. It's not easy to let go of a lifetime of resentment, but I'm working on it." She'd even visited him a few times in prison. "His coming to my rescue, knowing the men would kill him, was huge. I knew he'd do it for Kris, but never thought he'd do it for either Alyssa or me." His heartfelt apology had helped, too.

She sighed. "Kris is struggling, though. She's always idolized him, and this has devastated her. I hope she can eventually come to grips with everything."

"It has to be hard for her."

At least they wouldn't be fighting about selling the business. Kris had been getting more involved, taking some of the pressure off Kassie. Also, the finances were likely to be healthier than she'd anticipated. The police still had possession of the cash they found in the house, but all the bills were unmarked. So far, no one had come up with proof linking them to a crime, so the money would likely be returned. Kassie planned to pay off the loan on the Cabo, put some funds into marketing the business and stash the rest in savings.

Kassie had gone back to working at her salon a few days a week. But she wasn't about to give up her unofficial position as Buck's sometimes first mate, and she accompanied him at least once or twice a week.

There'd been one recent task she'd been happy to pass off— accounting. She and Kris had hired a part-time office person who happened to have a strong financial background.

Jared set aside his empty plate and waited for her to finish her last few bites. When she had, he slid onto the seat next to her and took both of her hands in his.

"As much as I love your sisters—at least the one I've met—I didn't plan this outing to talk about them. I brought you out here to talk about us."

"Us?" Kassie lifted her gaze to his face. For a relaxing, fun day on the water, he looked awfully serious.

Her pulse grew erratic, and a hollow sensation spread through her chest. Was he going to tell her they needed to cool it? Had he already decided he couldn't deal with her imperfections?

No, that was old insecurity creeping back to the surface. He'd never even hinted that he found fault with her.

Justice stood, lifted a paw and laid it in her lap.

She patted the top of his head. "Well, what's this about?"

"He's letting you know he chose you."

"For what?"

"To join the family."

She grinned "He did, did he?"

"Yep, a long time ago. Wouldn't take no for an answer. I told you he was a smart dog. Smarter than his master, apparently, because it took *him* a lot longer. But even *I* figure things out eventually."

Her heart beat so hard, it was pounding in her throat. He wasn't breaking up with her. He was going to ask her to marry him.

He squeezed her hands. "I didn't know I could ever feel this way about someone again. But over the past few months, I've fallen so much in love with you—your sweet nature, your strong faith, your strength and drive, your beautiful smile. I want you to be a permanent part of my life. Will you marry me?"

She swallowed hard. She'd believed she could never be what Jared needed, that she'd never live up to the memory of his dead wife.

She'd been wrong.

Miranda would always be in his heart. When a man loved as deeply as Jared did, that love never died.

But now she held that love, and what a gift it was.

Jared waited, doubt creeping across his features. Even Justice seemed to be waiting with bated breath.

She squeezed Jared's hands in return. "I love you too, everything about you. Yes, I'll marry you."

He released her hands to wrap his arms around her, then captured her mouth with his.

Justice went nuts, one excited bark after another. The dog had seen Jared kiss her many times, but he somehow sensed this one was different. Something important had transpired.

Something good.

Kassie couldn't agree more.

*   *   *   *   *

*If you enjoyed this story
by Carol J. Post,
don't miss the next book in the
Canine Defense series!*

*Coming soon from
Love Inspired Suspense.*

Discover more at LoveInspired.com

Dear Reader,

I hope you've enjoyed Kassie and Jared's story. This is the first book in the new Canine Defense series set in Pensacola, Florida.

Kassie and Jared were fun characters for me to write. Kassie endured a lot of criticism in her life and had to learn to see herself the way God sees her—as special and precious in His sight. Jared had a difficult time moving past the sudden loss of his wife and held a lot of regret. Both had to rely on God for healing from past traumas in order to find their happily-ever-after.

Be on the lookout for the next book in the series, where Kris finds love again. The final book will be Alyssa's story.

May God richly bless you in all you do.

Love in Christ,
Carol J. Post